Jack Lasenby was born in Waharoa, New Zealand in 1931. During the 1950s he was a deer culler and possum trapper in the Urewera Country. He is a former school teacher, lecturer in English at the Wellington Teachers' College, and editor of New Zealand's *School Journal*.

Jack Lasenby held the Sargeson Fellowship in 1991, the Writer's Fellowship at the Victoria University of Wellington in 1993, and was the Writer in Residence at the Dunedin College of Education in 1995. He is the author of many novels for children and young adults, including award-winning books *The Lake, The Conjuror, The Waterfall, The Battle of Pook Island* and *Taur*. He has been the recipient of New Zealand's most prestigious children's fiction awards: the Esther Glen Medal, the Aim Children's Book Award, and the NZ Post Children's Book Award.

Also by Jack Lasenby

The Lies of Harry Wakatipu

Jack Lasenby

"Not a word he says is true."

from *Memoirs of a Noble Packhorse,* by H. Wakatipu, Esq.

Longacre Press

© Jack Lasenby

ISBN 1 877135 41 0

First published by Longacre Press 2000,
9 Dowling Street, Dunedin, New Zealand.

Book and cover design by Christine Buess
Cover illustration by Bob Kerr
Printed by Australian Print Group

Contents

With Love for Jessie

Introduction
A Mean Spirit

In the time I'm talking about, the Vast Untrodden Ureweras used to stretch from just this side of Auckland to just this side of Wellington. They also took in the better part of the South Island, Stewart Island, the Chatham Islands, and what looks like empty space between us and South America. New Zealand hadn't shrunk in those days. Everything was twice as big. It took ten times as long to get there and was more fun.

When I ran away from home I went deer culling. I didn't think my mother could find me in the Vast Untrodden Ureweras. The field officer at Ruatahuna took me on but said I was too young to go into the bush without a mate. "You can take Harry Wakatipu," he said. "He'll be better company than a deer culler."

Deer were a curse in the bush, and the government paid a handful of tough jokers to shoot them out. We were the deer cullers, modest, laconic, taciturn. We weren't supposed to look at mirrors in case it turned us queer. We weren't allowed off our blocks. Broken legs we set ourselves. Bad cuts we cobbled together with a sacking needle. If we were really crook and had to go into Rotorua to the doctor, the field officer made us wear blinkers. They stop you from looking at your reflection in shop windows, and you can't see girls.

7

Rule Three in the Deer Culler's Daybook said, "Deer cullers have to suffer loneliness and hardship. They must not be told about girls and should sleep with their hands tied behind their backs." Unzipping a sleeping bag with your hands tied behind your back was too much trouble. We slept in the snow without sleeping bags. Rule Three also said, "Only sissies use tents."

After my voice broke I gave up tying my hands behind my back. Somebody reported me to the field officer who fined me a hundred bullets. If I've told Harry Wakatipu once, I've told him a thousand times he has a mean spirit.

Harry Wakatipu was supposed to be a pack-horse, but he refused to pack anything. He wouldn't chop firewood. He couldn't light a fire. He didn't know how to make a billy of tea. All he was good for was lying around the Hopuruahine hut, swigging condensed milk, and answering back.

For a while a well-educated boar pig called Biff Piddington carried my pack for me, but Harry Wakatipu drove him away. Then Wiki came, the best storyteller the Ureweras ever heard. Harry Wakatipu got rid of her, too. He wouldn't do a hand's turn around the place, but he didn't want anyone else doing it either. The only good thing was that Biff and Wiki sent messages in bottles down the Hopuruahine River saying they'd be back some day.

He's mean, he pongs, and he tells lies. I don't blame you for despising Harry Wakatipu.

Chapter One
How My Mother Stopped the Hopuruahine River

Two bottles came bobbing and glinting down the Hopuruahine River. The field officer was scared of the ford so he used to throw our mail into the head of the river, and we fished it out when it came past the Hopuruahine hut. I climbed down to collect the bottles, but Harry Wakatipu shoved past. He always has to be first. He has to read my mother's letters first. He has to have first slice when I bake bread. When we have a birthday party in the Hopuruahine hut, he has to have first go at blowing out the candles whether it's his birthday or not. "Look after Number One!" Harry Wakatipu always says.

Shoes ringing on the shingle, neighing "Ha! Ha!" he cantered across and snatched up the bottles. As he pulled out both corks with his teeth I recognised my mother's writing on the labels and dived down the back of a sand-bank. The explosion shook the valley for a couple of hours. The Hopuruahine River disappeared. So did Harry Wakatipu.

My mother had stuffed the bottles full of her home-made dynamite, stuck on stamps, and posted them to me. One thing I'll say for her, my mother's got a hard-case sense of humour.

I carried Harry Wakatipu's old saddle-blanket outside on the tip of my rifle barrel. I burnt the stinking hook-grass off his bunk. I swept out the hut and aired it to get rid of the pong of horse.

Under his bunk were a couple of my mother's letters he'd never shown me. One had a few grains of itching powder left in the envelope. I pitched it in the fire and remembered the time I got back and found Harry Wakatipu scratching himself. He'd fallen for another of my mother's little tricks.

The other letter said, "Congratulations! You have won ten million pounds. Bring this key to the Waharoa post office and unlock Private Box number 9." There was no key in the envelope so Harry Wakatipu must have fallen for that one, too. I could just see my mother crouching inside Private Box number 9, waiting to give me a hiding for running away. Harry Wakatipu would have cried out his name, but I'll bet my mother thrashed him all the harder, thinking it was me dressed up as a pack-horse.

I smiled grimly and heard something climbing down over the boulders where the Hopuruahine Cascades once roared. A white-tipped tail turned around and around, balancing its owner. I saw her white feet, her brown body, the white ruff around her neck, the white apron of hair on her chest. Wiki the storytelling dog was back!

She leapt and licked my face. Just in time I remembered Rule Three in the Deer Culler's Daybook and dropped her.

"Welcome home, Wiki," I said and shook hands in case the field officer was spying. If he'd seen me hug Wiki I'd have got the sack. Rule Three says, "A deer culler never shows his feelings."

"There's a brew on," I said gruffly. Wiki danced. It was all right for her to show her feelings because she was a dog. I held my upper lip stiff with both hands in case the field officer was watching through field glasses.

Each morning Wiki got up first and lit the fire. She did the cooking, carried my pack, and kept me company fly-camping. Each night she told me a story. I had to be careful not to go around with a silly grin on my face. Rule Three says, "A deer culler is allowed only three grins a season. He may laugh only if it stops him crying."

Several months later I was sitting on the doorstep drinking a mug of tea. Wiki was baking bread. I was so pleased to have her back I almost cried but remembered Rule Three. "What's that noise?" asked Wiki.

"I just sniffed."

"Haven't you got a hanky?" Wiki came to the door and listened.

I heard a noise like a bottle filling. A skinny string of blue water trickled down, filled a hole in the river-bed, and ran to the next. It started filling the pool below the waterfall. Six months later, the first water reached the lake, and you could say the Hopuruahine River was back. It was a good couple of years, though, before it rose to its old level. My mother's home-made dynamite was pretty strong stuff.

Chapter Two
The Scottish Traveller

We fly-camped up the Tundra, over the Ruakituri, and across the Waimana into the Whakatane. We poached the other deer cullers' blocks. While we sneaked into their camps and flogged their condensed milk, they sneaked into our camps and flogged our condensed milk. They also read our tracks, and word got around that Wiki the storytelling dog was back.

Suddenly the Hopuruahine was full of visitors. Possum trappers from the Southern Ureweras came hissing into the hut for a brew. The Dry Creek hermit limped in with one big toe in his hand. As I sewed it back on, he reckoned it had been bitten off by a mosquito, but I couldn't see any toothmarks. I think he chopped it off himself just so he could see Wiki. Disoriented surveyors called in for directions. Wildlife rangers stumbled in led by confused Labrador dogs. Garrulous high country musterers appeared with silent eye-dogs. Scarred pig hunters with loquacious holding-dogs. Even a couple of Forestry timber cruisers strayed out of the pines on the Kaingaroa Plain and ended up at the Hopuruahine.

We'd just get back from fly-camping, and the hut would begin to fill with strong silent men. Gumdiggers from the kauri forests of the Northern Ureweras, with climbing irons buckled on bare feet; moonshiners from the High Huiaraus whose whisky is so unstable it explodes below ten thousand feet; whalers from the western end of Lake Waikaremoana where they live in snow houses and marry seals.

These shy fellows all felt in their pockets and pulled out presents for Wiki. Humming birds fossilised inside lumps of kauri gum. Petrified whisky. Ivory coins carved out of the tusks of the extinct Lake Waikaremoana sperm whale. Night after night, the tough-gutted bushmen leaned laconic around the walls of the hut, and listened to Wiki's stories.

It happened one day about noon, going towards the river, I was exceedingly surprised with the print of a horse's hoof, which was very plain to be seen in the sand. I knew only one horse with such big feet, but said nothing to Wiki.

We went out for a shot in the afternoon, but the kakas were shrieking a storm warning, and we cut home down the river-bed. The footprint was still there, so clear we could see the nail-holes in the horny rim of the hoof, so it couldn't be a wild horse. Wiki said nothing, just lashed her tail.

Before dark the field officer arrived from Ruatahuna, pack-horses loaded with cases of ammunition, tealeaves, and condensed milk, a couple of grubby copies of the *Woman's Weekly*, and a letter from my mother. "Thought you might be running low on ammo," the field officer said. I'd often go a year or two without a visit from him. Usually he dumped my stores the other side of the dangerous ford above the Cascades and scuttled back to Ruatahuna. For some reason he insisted on carrying this lot inside. When he saw Wiki he blushed and made a bit of a fool of himself.

Wiki swung the big camp oven off the fire. "Wrap your laughing gear around this," she said, and everyone helped themselves to venison stew. For several hours the only sound was hungry men gutsing their tucker. They lit pipes, filled their mugs with tea and lashings of condensed milk, and stared silent into the fire. The wind shifted and carried the roar of the river; hail rattled in the chimney; snow sifted through the hole in the door where Harry Wakatipu once fired my rifle.

"Once upon a time…" said Wiki, and the honest fellows put down their mugs unfinished. Their mouths dropped open. Pipes clattered to the floor.

Wiki paused. "Go on," said a post splitter with a bandaged foot, but there was a knock, and a stranger entered. He wore a bowler hat, a swanny, and a kilt so long it hid his feet. Smoked glasses and a curly beard covered his nose and eyes. His sporran hung behind like a hairy tail. He said he was a Scottish traveller and grinned around saying, "Och, aye," and "Hoots, mon!" I nodded at the billy, and the stranger filled his mug made from an old Highlander milk tin and stirred in several tablespoons of condensed milk. Wiki was staring at the floor. I thought I saw wet hoof prints, but they dried and disappeared as I looked.

"Once upon a time," Wiki began again, "an Invercargill White slave trader sailed into Lake Waikaremoana."

"Och, aye!" sneered the Scottish traveller. "And what's an Invercargill White slave trader?" He swigged something from a bottle labelled "Old Pakaru Very Genuine Scotch Whisky".

"White slave traders," said Wiki, "kidnap young deer cullers, spray them with concrete, and sell them to Aucklanders as garden gnomes. They last for years."

"The Invercargill White slave trader landed and set traps for the young deer cullers, baited with condensed milk."

"Hoots, mon!" The Scottish traveller dropped and broke his bottle. Instead of whisky, condensed milk oozed across the floor. Everyone in the hut knew there was only one person in the Ureweras who drank it straight. Wiki bit the Scottish traveller. His kilt came off in her teeth. His dark glasses, his false beard, and his swanny came off. It was Harry Wakatipu.

The bushmen were angry with him for spoiling their story. They threw him on a blanket and tossed him so high there was a lunar eclipse. All you could hear was the rattle of moreporks bumping into trees in the dark. Harry Wakatipu flew past the moon, and its light shone again. He sailed higher, punched a hole in the sky, and disappeared. Tonight, if you look to the right of the second pointer to the Southern Cross, you can still see the horse-shaped black hole Harry Wakatipu made.

We had a brew and quietened down but it was time to crawl into our scratchers, so we never heard the rest of Wiki's story about the Invercargill White slave trader. Next morning I said to her, "How did you know the Scottish traveller was Harry Wakatipu?"

"I saw his hoof under his kilt," she replied. "It was the same shape as that footprint we saw."

16

Harry Wakatipu turned up a few years later with some cock and bull story about aliens who took him up in a flying saucer and dropped him from so high he fell right through the earth and came out in China. Harry Wakatipu's the biggest liar the Vast Untrodden Ureweras have ever seen – not like Wiki. Her stories are true.

Chapter Three

Harry Wakatipu and the Shorter Oxford English Dictionary

It was years before the Hopuruahine River returned to its full size. Several more passed, and Harry Wakatipu still wasn't back. I hoped he'd been tossed out past the sun. It was great having Wiki back at the Hopuruahine. I could have listened to her stories all day if I didn't have to get out and shoot deer. One day we got back from fly-camping on Whakatakaha and found a note from the field officer.

"I've burned all the tails on your line," he wrote, "and filled the tucker cupboard with condensed milk. There's a birthday present from your mother on your bunk."

I was suspicious of my mother's birthday presents and always left them lying around for Harry Wakatipu to open. He could never mind his own business so he got nipped when she posted a Black Widow spider; he got bitten by the rattle snake that jumped out of one of her birthday cards; and he was stung by the scorpion she sent me for Christmas. One year he opened a box addressed to me and saying "Happy birthday from your loving mother." Out poured hundreds of black and yellow insects, like bees but much angrier. They had a whale of a time stinging Harry Wakatipu, then flew through the rest of the country stinging everyone including my mother who was very annoyed. That was how the first wasps got into New Zealand.

Harry Wakatipu still wasn't back from China when my mother's birthday present arrived so I hid behind a tree, reached around with my skinning knife tied to the end of a stick, and cut it open. I was expecting one of my mother's little surprises, but no poisonous spider crawled out, no snake coiled and struck, no scorpion arched. Instead there were two huge volumes inside the parcel, the *Shorter Oxford English Dictionary on Historical Principles*. My mother had written, "Many happy returns of the day," inside the first volume. I reached with my long stick and opened the second volume, and it didn't blow up either. Somehow my mother had forgotten to put in one of her little surprises.

I still didn't trust her. Wiki found some mirrors hidden under Harry Wakatipu's bunk and we rigged them so I could read the words in the dictionary without being blown up. It was a very good dictionary. In the end I forgot about Mum and just opened and read it. I quite like words, especially those that describe Harry Wakatipu.

Like that word hypochondriac. Harry Wakatipu always thinks he's sick if the littlest thing goes wrong. When he came back from China complaining of a headache, I told him, "You're a hypochondriac, Harry Wakatipu."

"What's a hypochondriac?"

"You're a hypochondriac."

"What do you mean?"

"You've always got something wrong with you."

"I've got a headache."

"You're imagining it."

"You'd have a headache, too, if you'd fallen headfirst through the earth and come out in China."

"Don't tell stories, Harry Wakatipu."

"It's all right for that dog to tell stories but not for me."

"That's because you're an old hypocrite."

"What's a hypocrite?"

"You're a hypocrite."

"What do you mean?"

"It means you're a bombastical bombinator!"

"Where are you getting these long words from?" he asked.

Actually I'd found hypocrite in my dictionary, on the page after hypochondriac, just as I'd found bombinator after bombastic but I wasn't going to tell Harry Wakatipu. "Everyone knows what a hypocrite is," I said and thought I'd better shut up or he might start searching and find my dictionary in the hollow rata behind the hut. One day I brought the two volumes down and hid them in the foot of my sleeping bag. Harry Wakatipu wouldn't look in there.

A few days after that, Wiki told one of her stories, and Harry Wakatipu got jealous and tried to tell one, too.

"You'd better increase your vocabulary if you want us to listen to your stories," a post splitter told him.

"What do you mean?"

"Get yourself a dictionary and swallow it. That's the

20

way to learn big words."

Harry Wakatipu looked at me suspiciously. "That's what you've been doing," he said. "You swallowed a dictionary."

He didn't even know what a dictionary was. I ignored him and forgot about the two-volume *Shorter Oxford English Dictionary On Historical Principles* in the foot of my sleeping bag. I kept lots of things down there: old socks, a spare bush singlet, somebody's worn-out swanny, a promising pup, and a few rounds of ammunition. When the condensed milk got low in the tucker cupboard, I used to hide the last few tins in the foot of my sleeping bag so Harry Wakatipu wouldn't drink them all before the field officer brought fresh supplies. That was probably my undoing.

One night Wiki was telling a story when Harry Wakatipu said, "I can't hear the dog for your borborygms."

I didn't think I'd heard him clearly. "What's that?"

"Borborygms are stomach rumblings. You ate too much for tea, and I can't hear Wiki for your borborygms."

Everybody in the hut looked at me and laughed, and Wiki stopped telling her story.

"Go on, Wiki," I said and tried to smile, but my stomach rumbled very loud. I coughed to try and cover it.

"Heh, heh, heh!" said Harry Wakatipu in his nasty way.

"Shut up!" I told him. "I want to listen to the story."

"So do I, but I can't hear it for old Borborygmous here!"

Everyone laughed again. Fortunately Wiki went on with her story, and I sucked in my stomach so it was quiet.

I wondered where he was learning these big words but didn't think any more about it. Then one day he said, "During the matutinal hours I observed a marsupial ingesting the foliage of a Nothopanax arboreum"

I hadn't forgiven him for making fun of me in front of everybody. "You mean this morning you saw a possum eating five-finger leaves," I said. Later I thought about it. Where was he getting these big words?

Another night he tried to impress us with some big words while Wiki was telling a story. One of the surveyors asked him, "Have you swallowed a dictionary?"

I looked and saw Harry Wakatipu's eyes roll until they flashed white. They always did that when he was telling a lie. "No," he said.

I looked at once. Both volumes had disappeared from the foot of my sleeping bag. "Where's my dictionary?" I asked.

"I ate it," said Harry Wakatipu.

"Why?"

"Because that's easier than learning it one word at a time."

"You ate my dictionary?"

"I thought it would increase my vocabulary."

"You are an idiot, Harry Wakatipu." I listened and heard a strange sound.

Harry Wakatipu saw me looking and moved away, but I followed him. "It's you!" I said. "That was your guts rumbling because you swallowed my dictionary. Got the borborygms, have you, Harry Wakatipu. Well, it serves you right. I've warned you about my mother's little surprises.

"Don't look to me for sympathy," I told him. "I can't think of anything harder to digest than the *Shorter Oxford English Dictionary On Historical Principles,* unless it's the *Longer Oxford Dictionary On Historical Principles."*

"Oh, shut up!" he said.

"I didn't hear that."

"I said, 'Shut up!'"

"That's it!" I told him. "Out you go! And don't come back till you've digested that dictionary and you're a little less liverish."

"I am not liverish!" said Harry Wakatipu.

"It sounds to me," I said, "as if you might need a spoonful of Castor Oil." Harry Wakatipu can't stand Castor Oil. Just the sight of the blue bottle makes him feel sick. He galloped out of the hut and I put the bottle away. I don't like Castor Oil either. Just the look of the bottle reminds me of when I was little and my mother used to give me a spoonful every Saturday night.

I'm not letting him back in the hut, not till he apologises properly for being so rude. I'm the deer culler, after all. He's just the pack-horse. You wouldn't think so, the way he answers me back. I wonder if Castor Oil's in the *Shorter Oxford English Dictionary?* I'll never know, not now Harry Wakatipu's swallowed it.

Chapter Four
Riding to School

A blizzard thumped the valley. Snow was up to the roof of the Hopuruahine hut. I stared into the fire. Since Harry Wakatipu swallowed my dictionary there was nothing to read. Then Wiki the storytelling dog spoke. "Once upon a time," she said, "there were elephants in the Ureweras." I sat forward to hear, and somebody down the back of the hut said, "Huh!"

"Nowadays," said Wiki, "the kids ride horses to school. In the olden days we rode elephants. Every school had an elephant paddock. In time they became horse paddocks, and then footy fields, then they tar-sealed them to park the teachers' cars.

"Huh!"

"There were twenty-one kids in our family. We sat on our elephant in single file with our legs sticking out. I was the youngest so I sat at the back. When the elephant climbed uphill I kept sliding off."

"Huh!"

"Our elephant's name was Portugal. When she heard me cry she lifted me back up with her trunk."

"Huh!"

"Harry Wakatipu, I wish you'd stop saying, 'Huh!' I can't remember what I'm going to say next."

"Huh!"

"If you're not interested in hearing Wiki's story," I told him, "you'd better clear out."

Harry Wakatipu has an unpleasant habit of sneering and flapping his lips. "How could an elephant lift up someone who's fallen off their other end?" he asked. "Their trunks aren't that long!" He sneered, flapped his lips again, and said, "Huh!"

"Urewera elephants had a trunk at each end," Wiki said. "When I fell off Portugal picked me up with her back trunk.

"I've heard of African elephants and Asian elephants," said Harry Wakatipu, "but who's ever heard of Urewera elephants?" He sneered, flapped his lips, and looked around. There was a crowd of deer cullers, our cowardly field officer, half a dozen possum trappers, several post splitters, a couple of shearing gangs, and a surveyor's team in the Hopuruahine hut that night.

"Besides," said Harry Wakatipu, "how could an elephant with a trunk at each end go to the dunny?"

"Over in the Horomanga," said one of the possum trappers, "I've seen tracks big enough to be an elephant's."

A surveyor spat in the fire. "I knew a girl in Te Whaiti," he said. "She reckoned her Aunty Kahu saw elephants over in the Ruakituri."

"Huh!" said Harry Wakatipu. "Nobody's ever been over in the Ruakituri. Everyone's too scared of it."

Wiki and I often fly-camped the Ruakituri but I didn't daren't say so because the field officer would sack me. I wasn't supposed to go over there because he reckoned I'd get lost.

26

"Now I think of it," I said, "I've heard some funny noises from my camp on Manuoha. It could have been elephants trumpeting down in the Ruakituri."

"Did they sound as if they had two trunks?"

"Funny you should ask that. They went, 'Ta-raah, ta-raah!'"

"'Ta-raah, ta-raah' doesn't sound like two-trunked elephants trumpeting to me," said Harry Wakatipu. "Huh!"

"Do you want to hear this story or not?" asked Wiki.

"Let the little dog tell her story, Donkey," said a deep voice. The floor creaked, and a huge shadow moved out of the night and into the Hopuruahine hut. I threw a log on the fire. Flames lit white a single tusk that curved out of the bottom jaw of a giant boar pig.

"Biff Piddington!" My voice wobbled. "Oh, Biff, you've come back!" I sat him in his old seat beside my chair in front of the fire. I gave him a billy of tea, a camp oven full of stew, a loaf of bread I'd just baked, and his old spoon, his favourite one. "Wiki was just telling us a story."

Biff put one gigantic trotter around my shoulder and nodded to the silent listeners. "I was postponing my entrance," he said, "despite the inclement weather outside. I did not wish to intrude while Wiki was recounting her anecdote. But you," he said to Harry Wakatipu, "have disrupted her narrative with that offensive sneer. Shut up, Donkey, or I'll rip a tusk into you!" He scoffed his huge tusk on its grinder so it showered sparks. The hut stunk with Harry Wakatipu's singed hair and the pong he gives off when scared.

Harry Wakatipu hates being called a donkey. He scrambled on to the top bunk, turned his face to the

27

wall and grizzled. Wiki sat up on her stool and grinned.

"Once upon a time," she said, "there were elephants all through the Ureweras, special Urewera elephants with a trunk at each end. Ours was called Portugal and we rode her to school. At playtime, all the elephants held each other's trunks and made skipping ropes for us. Portugal could join both ends of her two trunks and jump through them herself. She could do Salt-Mustard-Vinegar-Pepper faster than anybody in the Vast Untrodden Ureweras.

"The day of the School Picnic, there was going to be a lolly scramble and cream buns for lunch. We rode Portugal to school, all twenty-one of us. The dangerous Hopuruahine ford was in flood. It was too deep for Portugal to swim, so she picked up a boulder with her front trunk, to keep her feet on the bottom, and walked across under water. We had to stand on tiptoe to breathe."

"How did Portugal breathe?" asked one of the post splitters.

"She stuck her back trunk out of the water and breathed through that. We had almost reached the far side when there was a terrible roar. A crocodile came swimming down the river, all its jaws wide open. It was going to swallow us in one colossal bite, all twenty-one of us."

"Huh!" Harry Wakatipu's long head hung over the top bunk. "Since when have there been crocodiles in the Hopuruahine?" He flapped his lips together and sneered knowingly.

"In the olden days," said Wiki, "there were crocodiles all through the bush. Urewera crocodiles with a head at each end."

"It's true!" said the possum trapper who'd tramped all the way from the other side of the bush to hear Wiki's story. "I'm having trouble with two-headed crocodiles taking the possums out of my traps in the Horomanga River."

"Have you actually seen one?" asked Harry Wakatipu.

"I've seen their tracks," said the trapper. "You know the spring on a Lane's Ace trap? Well these two-headed crocodiles can straighten it out flat with one bite!" The other possum trappers looked at each other in horror.

Harry Wakatipu looked as if he might sneer and flap his lips together, but Biff Piddington grumbled, "Let the little dog finish her story, Donkey." We all leaned forward and listened.

"The crocodile roared and opened its jaws so wide we could smell its bad breath. We were going to miss the School Picnic, the lolly scramble, and the cream buns. We all cried."

Wiki shivered on her stool. Her ears were laid back. Her tail lashed from side to side. She was remembering that day in the Hopuruahine ford.

"Portugal bucked us off so we landed in a row on the bank, all twenty-one of us. She grabbed the crocodile by one head with her front trunk as it bit her back trunk with its other head. Neither would let go. Roaring and trumpeting, they rolled down the flooded river like a wet black tyre going round and round.

"Halfway down the gorge below the Cascades, a wave tossed Portugal and the crocodile high in the air. It flung them like a bangle over a tree. The tree fell across the river. Neither Portugal nor the crocodile would let go.

They starved to death, locked in a circle around the log. Their skeletons are still there today."

"How do you know?" said Harry Wakatipu. "Nobody's gone down the Cascades and lived."

"I believe every word, Wiki," said Biff Piddington.

"Some day," said Harry Wakatipu, "I'm going to invent an aeroplane with a propeller at each end so it can fly backwards and forwards and up and down. And I'll fly through the Hopuruahine gorge and see if your story's true."

"I'd like an aeroplane like that," said the cowardly field officer who was scared to cross the Hopuruahine ford because of crocodiles. "What's it called?"

"A Whirligig," said Harry Wakatipu. He mumbled something else, but the silent men were all getting into their sleeping bags. Snow and sleet lashed the Hopuruahine hut. The river roared in its gorge.

"Elephants with trunks at each end!" Harry Wakatipu said. "Crocodiles with two heads!"

"Donkey!" said Biff Piddington threateningly. He had crawled under my bunk to sleep. I stuck my hand down and patted his coarse black bristles. "Welcome home," I whispered.

"My Whirligig aeroplane," said Harry Wakatipu, "could fly up and down and backwards and forwards like a double helix. Helix," he repeated. "Helical... Helico..."

"Shut up!" everyone said, but Harry Wakatipu talked on, showing off his vocabulary.

"Then there's that Greek word, *pteron*, for a wing. I know! I'll join them together and make a new word for my invention. I'm going to call it a *Helicopteron*!"

"Oh, shut up!" everyone told Harry Wakatipu. "Go to sleep."

He only knew those words because he swallowed the dictionary my mother sent for my birthday present. Harry Wakatipu only knew how to read because I taught him. He wasn't really interested in making up words.

"Helicopteron," I whispered to Biff Piddington. "It doesn't sound quite right. "I know! Helicopter! That's the word they'll use when they build an aeroplane like that."

"Don't tell the donkey," whispered Biff Piddington. "Or he'll say he thought of it." He cleared his throat.

"Helicopteron," Biff Piddington said clearly so everyone in the hut could hear him. "Whoever heard of a word like that? Harry Wakatipu does not comprehend the first principles of lexicology."

I listened and smiled to myself. We were all back together at the Hopuruahine hut again, me, Wiki, Biff Piddington. And Harry Wakatipu.

Chapter Five
Clancy's Whip

We were talking about whips, one night in the Hopuruahine hut. Wiki, the storytelling dog, reckoned she had seen the world's greatest whip-cracker in action.

"In the last century," she said, "the Horomanga River ran into the Hauraki Gulf at Thames, and the big square-riggers sailed right up to Murupara to load out the clip from Galatea Station. They carted the bales to the wharves on hundred-wheeled wagons."

"Hundred-wheeled wagons?" Harry Wakatipu scoffed.

"The bales were ten times bigger than they are today," said Wiki. "The sheep were the size of a horse."

Harry Wakatipu snorted. "Sheep as big as horses?"

"In those days," Wiki said, "a big ram would put away a couple of pack-horses for breakfast, no trouble."

Harry Wakatipu swallowed. "All the same," he said. "Who's ever seen a wagon with a hundred wheels?" Nobody answered him. "Get on with your story," he said in his disagreeable way.

"When I was a pup," said Wiki, "the North Island started shrinking, the Horomanga River silted up, and the big square-riggers couldn't sail up to Murupara. The sheep got smaller, and the shearers pressed wool in the little bales we know today. My father was shearing on Galatea and showed me the last of those hundred-wheeled wagons, standing under a macrocarpa hedge. For ninety years leaves and twigs had piled up in its bed. Its wheels had sunk up to the axles in the ground. Loaded five-high with giant bales of wool, it took two hundred and seventy-eight draught-horses to shift it, my father said."

It was a wild winter's night at the Hopuruahine hut. A couple of drovers, half a dozen shearers, the field officer, and nine deer cullers – including myself, Biff Piddington, and Harry Wakatipu – were sitting in front of the fire listening to Wiki's story. She stopped and looked around our faces.

"Go on!" said Harry Wakatipu. I wished Wiki hadn't mentioned those horse-eating sheep. He'd probably have a nightmare tonight, and I'd have to get up and warm him a tin of condensed milk or nobody would get any sleep. I looked at Wiki and shook my head, but she looked away.

She took a mouthful of tea and put down her mug. "There was an Aussie, a shortish chap, Freddy Stromboli, in the gang. He fancied himself as a gun shearer but couldn't keep up to my father. At smoke-oh, one morning, he said he'd heard my father was a dab hand with a stock whip and challenged him to see who could crack one loudest.

"Now, when Clancy died he left his famous whip to my great-grandmother, and it had come down to my father. He stood clear of the shed and swung Clancy's famous stock whip.

"The first time he cracked it the barbs fell off all the fences around Galatea. The second time, the corrugated iron on the shearing shed flattened out. The third time, the wax shot out of the ears of the pack-horses bringing the scones for smoke-oh and they dropped dead, all twenty-five of them."

Harry Wakatipu gulped loudly. "That's what I call whip-cracking!" said one of the drovers who'd called to hear Wiki's story.

"I think perhaps we'd all better go to bed now." I caught Wiki's eye and nodded at Harry Wakatipu. He had his hands over his eyes and was peering between them, white-faced.

"I don't think I like this story," he started to say, but Wiki took another sip from her mug and sat it to keep warm on the hearth.

"Freddy Stromboli swaggered out, just a little fellow, so short the shearers used him to open up the bellies. He could walk under a Merino wether without taking off his hat."

Harry Wakatipu snickered. He always liked hearing about people smaller than himself.

"His whip was forty feet long and trailed across the ground," said Wiki, "so some of the other shearers sneered."

"Heh, heh, heh!" sneered Harry Wakatipu.

"Freddy Stromboli strutted a few quick steps and picked up the body of the whip like a fly fisherman lifting his line off the river," said Wiki. "He made several false casts and pointed at the hundred-wheeled wagon under the macrocarpa hedge.

"Freddy Stromboli swore he'd move it out the gates of Galatea Station, turn it around, and bring it back and leave it under the macrocarpas where it had stood for ninety years, all just with his whip-cracking. "If I win," he said, "I get Clancy's whip. If I lose, I hand over my cheque."

"Fair enough," my father agreed. Everyone thought Freddy Stomboli had gone cuckoo and had a quid on it that he'd never shift the wagon.

"Stew Coupar was the head shepherd on Galatea Station in those days, and he held his old lemon-squeezer with all the bets. Freddy Stromboli danced and cracked his whip so hard the macrocarpa hedge burst into flames. The shearers shuffled uneasily as their eardrums burst. My father had stuck his fingers in my ears so I couldn't hear the swearing. That's the only reason I'm not deaf today.

"The old wagon shuddered. Its wheels rocked. Again Freddy Stromboli swung his massive stock whip, wound up, and wham! The Kaingaroa Forest fell over and people put it down to the Tarawera Eruption. Every chook from Murupara to Whakatane went off the lay, and the wagon wheels turned.

"Freddy Stromboli cracked his whip again and again, and that enormous old wagon heaved itself out of the ground and trundled out the gates of Galatea Station. The dry axles shrieked so loud every woodpecker this side of the Huiaraus took off for Australia. That's why today there's not a single New Zealand woodpecker north of Lake Waikaremoana."

"By God," said an old drover, looking at the stock whip hanging under his oilskins on the wall of the Hopuruahine hut. "That was whip-cracking!"

"Oh, I don't know," said Wiki. "Freddy Stromboli only got the wagon through the station gates and under the big poplar there before it pulled up. All the whip-cracking in the world wouldn't turn it round."

"He wasn't that good after all," said Harry Wakatipu.

"You might say that," said Wiki, "but you could say he wasn't bad, either."

Harry Wakatipu looked sideways. He was never sure if Wiki was having him on. "Is that a true story?" he asked.

"That big poplar," said Wiki, "outside where the gates of Galatea Station used to be?" Harry Wakatipu nodded. "Next time you're down in Murupara," said Wiki, "have a look in the long grass under that poplar. You'll find the irons off all the swingle-trees for hitching up two hundred and seventy-eight Clydesdales to pull that thundering great wagon, as well as a hundred iron wheel rims and all the brake shoes. Somebody must have flung the swingle-trees up into the bed of the wagon, the last time it was used. They rotted away with the woodwork where the wagon stood under the poplar after Freddy Stromboli lost his cheque."

"True?"

"Have a look for yourself."

The Hopuruahine hut was silent. Everyone turned in, everyone but Harry Wakatipu. He sat over the fire plaiting something.

Biff Piddington and I were coming off the ridge after a morning shoot, next day, and we saw Harry Wakatipu below on the river-bed, teaching himself to crack a whip. Boar pigs are short-sighted, so Biff watched through my field glasses. Harry Wakatipu got the full length of the whip flowing and flicked just a split-second too soon. On the end of the lash the cracker snapped back and took off his right ear. I couldn't have done it cleaner with my skinning knife.

Harry Wakatipu was lucky Biff was glassing him. We dropped down, found the ear, and I stitched it back on while Wiki told a story about how her grandmother saw Freddy Stromboli throw the discus. I had a word with her afterwards.

"You'd better watch what you say, Wiki. If Harry Wakatipu tries to throw the discus, he'll forget to let go and send himself flying instead."

There was a certain look on Wiki's face. I can't help wondering if she intended Harry Wakatipu to make a fool of himself with that stock whip. And I don't know that I believe her story about Freddy Stromboli either.

I left the bandage on Harry Wakatipu's ear for a few days. When I had a look, I got a bit of a shock. I'd been so busy listening to Wiki's story about Freddy Stromboli throwing the discus, I'd sewn the ear on back to front. I thought Harry Wakatipu would cry and carry on, but he wouldn't let me take it off and sew it on the other way.

Biff Piddington worked it out, why Harry Wakatipu wants to keep one ear pointing one way and one the other. He thinks we won't be able to sneak up on him when he's stealing condensed milk. You've got no idea what a liar and a thief he is, Harry Wakatipu.

Last time I was down at Murupara I rode out the old Galatea Station road and had a look under the big poplar this side of where the gates used to stand. Amongst the cocksfoot and tall fescue I kicked around and came up with a heap of swingle-tree irons, near rusted away, and scores of those iron rims off old wagon wheels. I didn't tell Harry Wakatipu. It's probably better if he's not sure whether Wiki's stories are true or not.

Chapter Six

How the Jug-Headed Wild Horses Came to the Kaingaroa Plains

News came to the Hopuruahine that the deer cullers' pack-train carrying condensed milk from Rotorua had been held up on the Kaingaroa Plains by wild horses. The thieves got off with a good three thousand cases. The government reacted quickly. From Thames to Murupara the Horomanga River was closed to all other shipping while emergency supplies were sailed in. Until they were packed through to Lake Waikaremoana we were going to have to ration ourselves.

"How do they expect me to live," Harry Wakatipu whined, "without my condensed milk?"

"It's not your condensed milk," I told him. "Rule Three in the Deer Culler's Daybook says 'one tin per man per day'. It says nothing about pack-horses."

"Donkey," Biff Piddington said, "exert a little self-control."

"Oh, shut up, Pig!" Harry Wakatipu scratched his side, compulsively.

We'd had our evening feed. I sprawled back in my chair, feet propped on the camp oven. Biff Piddington lay beside me like a small black hill. Harry Wakatipu slouched on an ammunition case. He'd been licking an empty condensed milk tin all day and was bumping his head against the tucker cupboard door. Bump. Bump. Bump.

"How did the jug-headed wild horses get on to the Kaingaroa in the first place?" I asked Wiki.

She sat on an empty condensed milk case, slanting her eyes at Harry Wakatipu. "Years back," she said, "an eruption from Tarawera burned the bush off that steep face of the Ureweras from the Hautapu hut all the way down behind Murupara to where the Horomanga comes out of the hills. Red tussock came up through the ashes, and Galatea Station ran long-legged merinos on it. The only way to muster them was on horseback.

"Stew Coupar was head shepherd on Galatea, and he used to start the mustering gang on Frying Pan Flat above the Hautapu hut. The bush was above on their right, the Rangitaiki River below on their left, so it was natural for the merinos to run north along the steep face. Of course the Vast Untrodden Ureweras were a bit bigger then. It was all of a thousand miles from the Hautapu hut to the woolshed, and the whole way you were walking on a left-handed slant. By the time they finished the muster, all the horses had dislocated hips on the uphill side.

"It took three years to muster, three years to shear, and three years to get the last of those merinos back out on the hills again. The shed on Galatea was so big, a sheep would go in a lamb and come out a full-grown two-tooth. But Stew Coupar's biggest problem was all those horses with dislocated hips. Mrs Galatea ordered

40

him to dog-tucker the lot."

Harry Wakatipu scratched his side and donged his head on the tucker cupboard door. Thump! Thump! Thump! Wiki looked at him and went on with her story.

"Stew refused to shoot those honest, hard-working nags," said Wiki. "He sent them to muster the station's cattle beasts off Tarawera Mountain, only he told them to go round it anti-clockwise, on a right-handed slant. It took three years. By that time their hips were okay for mustering the Urewera faces again. It was only a half-pie cure though and still left the station shy of horses.

"Stew wrote to a mate down the Hawke's Bay, Henry Rawiri. He put a thousand horses together and brought them up over the Napier-Taupo stock route. The idea was to turn off at the Rangitaiki pub, follow the Old Taupo Track through Te Ngaere Clearings to Te Whaiti, and swim the horses down the Whirinaki River to Galatea."

Harry Wakatipu was scratching, shaking his head from side to side, brushing his face with his front feet. Both eyes rolled in towards his nose, and their whites flashed.

"Biff!" I said. The enormous boar pig ripped the top off a tin of condensed milk and tipped it down the pack-horse's gullet. Biff held Harry Wakatipu's fetlock and said his pulse was slowing. His panting stopped. His head stopped shaking.

"The scratching and head-shaking," said Biff Piddington, "were withdrawal symptoms. Harry Wakatipu's mitochondrial count has now stabilised."

"Where do you get this language from?" I asked him.

"Where did you learn to take a pulse. And these what-do-call-them symptoms, where'd you hear about them?"

"In my youth," said Biff Piddington, "I qualified in medicine, but people didn't like the idea of a boar pig as their G.P. Forced out of practice I offered my services to the Rotorua hospital free of charge. Unfortunately the locals said they didn't like being treated by some-body with a hairy, black hide."

Harry Wakatipu sat up. "Who'd want to be treated by a pig?" he demanded.

"Biff Piddington just saved your life. You should be grateful."

"Grateful, Hateful!" said Harry Wakatipu. He always rhymes things when he's in that sort of mood. "Sees them, Pees them!" he said.

"You are a coarse donkey," said Biff Piddington. "Nevertheless, I must be true to my oath and bring healing where I can." He lay down again, and Wiki went on with her story.

"After a couple of years, Henry Rawiri reached the Mounted Constabulary fort at the head of the Rangitaiki River. It had been turned into a pub by his old mate, Mike Bennett. Henry left the horses guarded by his intelligent dogs and went in to say goodday to Mike."

"Why did the Mounted Constabulary build a fort up there?" I asked.

"Because Horse-Cannibals were holding up travellers on the Napier-Taupo stock route."

At the mention of Horse-Cannibals, Harry Wakatipu began flapping his feet, shaking his head, carrying on the way he had before.

Biff Piddington took his pulse, looked at his tongue, held a candle to his eyes. "Harry Wakatipu is faking withdrawal symptoms with the fraudulent intention of obtaining more condensed milk." he said. "Continue your narrative, Wiki."

Wiki yapped. She liked seeing Harry Wakatipu embarrassed. "Henry Rawiri and Mick Bennett got stuck into a barrel of Old Pakaru Whisky. They tossed it down with chasers of matai beer. Then Mrs Waerenga brought the boys in from her post-splitting camp. The shearers arrived from Poronui Station. The surveyors came in from Sixty Bar Eight. Two deer cullers trickled in, all the way from the Upper Te Hoe. It was a great old Saturday night at the Rangitaiki.

"Henry Rawiri woke next morning where he'd slept in the tussock. He put on his boots, walked off the way they were pointing into the Grim Inscrutable Ureweras, and was never seen again.

"His intelligent dogs rounded up the horses, and pushed them on. They didn't know Henry meant to turn off on the Old Taupo Track across the Rangitaiki, through Te Ngaere and the Waiatiu to Te Whaiti and down the Whirinaki to Galatea. They headed towards Rainbow Mountain.

"Now Earle Vaile had started breaking in that pumice country he called Broadlands, and he'd fenced off the Rotorua short-cut the drovers had used for centuries. The intelligent dogs kept the mob together till they met up with the fence where a couple of stallions got themselves badly wired. The horses broke out, galloped north, and parked up in a tussock basin. It suited them. The

Rangitaiki ran below on their right. The Kaingaroa Plains stretched forever around them. The Vast Untrodden Ureweras were a blue wall to the south and east.

"The mob had been on the road several years now, and there were a couple of thousand colts running with the mares. The intelligent dogs cut out the pick of them and ran them down the Rangitaiki to Murupara where Stew Coupar was in town picking up the mail. He paid off the head dog and said anyone who wanted a job on the station was welcome to stay.

The head dog split the cheque fair and square with his mates and married the pick of Stew Coupar's heading dogs, a strong-eyed bitch with a white-tipped tail and four white feet. After a brief honeymoon at Kiorenui Village beside the river they settled at Galatea Station.

"That head dog was my great-great-great-grand-father," said Wiki. "That strong-eyed bitch was my great-great-great-grandmother." A log stirred and crumbled to embers.

"That's a fine story, Wiki!" I exclaimed.

She nodded. "Stew Coupar drove the foals up the side of First Mimi Hill," she said. "He drafted out and bred from the ones who leaned to the right. After a few generations, he had a line of horses whose uphill legs were shorter than their downhill legs. They could muster the steep faces of the Ureweras good-oh. Ever since, people have bred from his Galatea strain when they want Urewera pack-horses."

"Supposing a quadruped's legs are short on the up-hill side," Biff Piddington said. "What happens when the animal is about to come down the other– "

Wiki butted into what he was saying, and I never heard the rest of Biff Piddington's question.

"One of the colts," Wiki said, "was the great-great-great-grandfather of a certain horse we all know. He already had a name for laziness. He was notorious for puffing himself up with wind. As soon as he was loaded he let out the air, and his pack-saddle slipped around and hung down between his legs. 'All he's good for,' Stew Coupar used to say, 'is dog tucker.'

"In those days," said Wiki, "Highlander condensed milk used to come in four-gallon jugs. The no-good colt was found one morning," said Wiki, "in the cookhouse, a jug stuck on his head. After that, they couldn't keep him away from the cookhouse."

"Hee haw! Hee haw! Hee haw!" Harry Wakatipu brayed. "He must have been my great-great-great-grand-father."

"You've guessed the end of my story," Wiki said. "And there's nothing wrong with you, you old fraud. I saw you putting it on, that business of feeling faint and shaking your head around. That's what your great-great-great-grandfather used to do outside the kitchen on Galatea Station, trying to win sympathy – and another jug of condensed milk.

"At last," she said, "Stew Coupar caught him again with a jug stuck on his head. Stew ordered the old thief to be dogged across the Rangitaiki River. He wandered round in the tussock and scrub, the jug stuck on his head, until he ganged up with a mob of Henry Rawiri's mares. Their descendants have lived there ever since. That," Wiki said, "is how the jug-headed wild horses came to the Kaingaroa."

Outside the wind carried the noise of the river from its gorge. It was going to snow before morning. Biff Piddington snored comfortably. Wiki dropped her head and slept on top of her box. I threw a log on the fire to keep it in and tossed a tin of condensed milk to Harry Wakatipu. We had enough to last us till the emergency supplies came through.

He winked and stuck out his right legs. "Look!" he whispered. Both legs were a bit shorter that side.

"You're just holding them so they look like that," I said. But they did look shorter. Even the hoofs seemed worn to the right. Maybe Wiki's story was true and Harry Wakatipu is descended from that condensed milk-stealing horse who came up the Napier-Taupo Track and across the Kaingaroa to the old Galatea Station. He's got the right-shaped head for it.

Chapter Seven
One Big Happy Family

The snotty-gobble tree behind the Hopuruahine hut tapped the wall. Hail rattled on the roof like somebody rolling Jaffas on the floor at the pictures. A door squeaked. I half-opened one eye.

Wiki lay asleep on my left, one ear pricked. Biff Piddington rested his colossal chin on my right foot. A snore escaped his ugly mouth as he munched on his single tusk. The other side of him, Harry Wakatipu slouched on his ammunition case, mouth open, dribble shining down his chin. I knew he had one hand inside the tucker cupboard. Wiki's ear stood up sharper. Biff growled something and snored again.

"Lay off it, Harry Wakatipu," I said. "We just had a feed, and you gutsed more than the rest of us put together. You don't need another tin of condensed milk already."

"I was just stretching my arms," he whined and pulled his hoof out of the cupboard. His eyes rolled till the whites of them flashed, a sure sign he was lying.

"Garbage-guts," said Wiki. "You were trying to nick a tin of cond."

"I was not!"

"You were so."

"I was not."

"Donkey, abandon this childish hunger for sweet sensations," said Biff Piddington. "I heard you groping in the tucker cupboard."

"Biff's right," I said. "Act your age."

"I need a high-calory diet. I'm a growing pack-horse."

"When was the last time you carried a pack?"

"I hate you all," said Harry Wakatipu. "That dog, I hate her. And you, you big pig, I hate you, too." He put his hands over his face and pretended to cry, but the whites of his eyes flashed again. "You always listen to them. It's not fair."

"The reason," Biff said in his reasonable way, "is that you are forever purloining condensed milk."

"I hate you all!"

Wiki grinned. "You're a liar, a thief, and you pong."

"I do not!"

"You do so!"

"It's blowing a blizzard outside," I said, "and we're safe inside the Hopuruahine hut. Why can't we all be content with what we've got? Why can't we just be one big happy family?"

"What would you know about happy families?" Harry Wakatipu muttered. "Who ran away from his poor old mother and his good home at Waharoa?"

Biff and Wiki looked at me.

"It's not the same," I said.

"You do not have to explain yourself," said Biff Piddington.

"You must have had a very good reason," said Wiki. "We're not curious."

There was a long pause. "Why did you run away from

48

home?" they asked together.

"So he wouldn't have to help around the house," Harry Wakatipu blabbed. "He refused to do a hand's turn. He wouldn't keep his room tidy. He told lies and picked his nose. He broke his poor old mother's heart."

The candle flickered. Snow blew in the bullet-hole Harry Wakatipu had made in the door. "How would you like to sleep outside?" I asked him.

"Get stuffed!"

"I didn't hear that!" I said quietly but firmly.

Harry Wakatipu said it again.

"Are you going to apologise, or do I have to put you outside?"

"Just because you're a deer culler you think you're the boss!"

"One more word from you," I said, "and out you go."

"It's not fair. I'm sick of being pushed round. Mungee mungee taipo!"

"Harry Wakatipu!"

"Big black devil!"

"That's terrible," I told him. "You mustn't say that."

"Mungee mungee taipo! Mungee mungee taipo!"

He lost all control. He jumped up and down, screaming. The more I tried to shut him up, the louder he yelled.

"You could get into trouble saying that."

"Big black devil!" Harry Wakatipu shouted all the louder. "Big black devil!"

"My mother told me it's rude to say 'mungee mungee taipo'," said Wiki. "It's offensive to Maoris."

Biff Piddington nodded his ponderous head. "I over-

49

heard Mrs Rawiri inform her mokopunas that the phrase is offensive to Pakehas."

"Whatever or whoever," I said, "you shouldn't say it, Harry Wakatipu. You could summon up the devil."

"Mungee mungee taipo," he shouted. The whites of his eyes flashed. "Big black devil!" And something thumped on the iron roof.

We looked at each other. And something thumped on the ground outside the door.

"Mungee mungee taipo!" shouted Harry Wakatipu, not so loud this time.

Something thumped on the door.

"Mungee mungee taipo," whispered Harry Wakatipu. I could hardly hear him now, just a scared little voice that whispered, "Big black devil!"

Something hurled itself against the door.

"You've done it this time, Harry Wakatipu. You summoned up the devil. You open the door before he kicks it down."

The door shook in its frame.

Harry Wakatipu tried to get behind Wiki. She dodged. He tried to get behind Biff's huge bulk, but the boar pig shoved him towards the door.

"Take your medicine," said Biff Piddington, "like a man."

"But I'm a pack-horse!"

We stood in a row, backs to the fire. Although it should have been hot, my neck felt icy. The hairs along Biff Piddington's spine stuck up like the bristles on a dunny brush. Wiki's ears were laid back, her lips lifted in a snarl. Something outside was pulling at the latch. I should leap

50

and slash the string before the door opened, but my fingers wouldn't close round the handle of my skinning knife. I couldn't pull it from its sheath. My feet wouldn't lift up from the floor It was like that dream where I can't run away from the Bogey-Man because my legs won't work.

It was Harry Wakatipu's fault. My mother always said we weren't allowed to say "Mungee mungee taipo". If we did, she washed out our mouths with soap, and we spat yellow bubbles for weeks.

The latch raised slowly. I tried to make my feet walk, tried to pull out my skinning knife. And Harry Wakatipu shrieked.

The latch lifted. The door banged open. The candle blew out. The firelight came from behind us so we stared helpless into the dark, and two, terrible, green eyes glared back.

"They said it, not me!" the cowardly pack-horse screamed and dived headfirst into my sleeping bag. The green eyes swayed closer.

Wiki and Biff were both trying to get behind me. I'd have got behind them but my feet wouldn't shift. Biff's black jaws moved as if praying. I tried closing my eyes but they opened themselves again. I said, "Our father which art in heaven" but couldn't remember any more of the words, and the green eyes came closer. Black snow swirled in the door. Wind scathed the floor. Harry Wakatipu screamed inside my sleeping bag, and I smelled the pong he gives off when he's scared.

"Ugh!" the devil said. "Not a fit night out for cat or beast." And it picked its way delicately into the hut,

51

scattering drops of water off its fur.

"*Man* or beast," Biff Piddington corrected it automatically. He had once been a school teacher.

"Who do you think you are?" asked the cat.

"Biff Piddington."

"Indeed! Well don't correct my English another time. When I say cat, I mean cat; and when I say pig, I mean pig."

The black cat jumped up on my chair. Harry Wakatipu moaned on my bunk, waiting for the devil to eat him.

"Tell him to pull his head out of that sleeping bag and get over here."

Biff pulled off the sleeping bag. Harry Wakatipu screamed.

"Did I hear you calling me a taipo?"

"It was him!" Harry Wakatipu pointed at me.

"It was your voice."

"I was just singing a little song," said Harry Wakatipu. "You know– " He clasped Biff and danced around the hut on his hind legs. "Mungee-mang, mungee-mang, taipopo, taipopo," he hummed in waltz time.

The cat rolled in my chair, laughing. Disgusted, Biff Piddington shoved Harry Wakatipu away and brushed himself down. Wiki grinned but kept one eye on the cat.

"And who are you?"

"The question is rather," said Wiki, "how dare you walk into the Hopuruahine hut and start asking questions?"

The cat yawned and licked one paw with a tongue as tiny as a pink moth. "I," she said, "am Hoho McKenzie."

"That's not what it says on your collar."

"Haven't we sharp eyes! My name is Hoho McKenzie, alias Gladys Tuhakaraina. Satisfied, Smartypants?"

I could see Wiki and Hoho McKenzie were not going to get on.

"What's alias?" asked Harry Wakatipu.

"It means," said Biff Piddington, "her name is Hoho McKenzie, but she is also known as Gladys Tuhakaraina."

"Why can't you make up your mind?" asked the pack-horse.

"My mind is made up," said Hoho. "It was my mother and father. They spent long hours arguing and reciting their genealogies– "

"What's geneographies?"

"Genealogy," said Biff Piddington. "It's a family tree."

"Why did your father spend so long climbing a tree?" Harry Wakatipu asked Hoho McKenzie.

"She is using a metaphor," Biff told him, "when she says 'family tree'. It does not mean her father climbed a real tree."

"She said he did."

"Shut up and listen," I told Harry Wakatipu. "You'll never hear the story if you keep asking questions."

"My name is Hoho McKenzie," said the cat, "also known as Gladys Tuhakaraina because all cats have nine names, but I won't bother you with the other seven. I was born in Waharoa in the Northern Ureweras. My mother was the Plunket Nurse and my father was Banana Bob, the Rawleighs Man. Mine is a tragic story."

I sat on Harry Wakatipu's ammunition case because Hoho McKenzie was sitting in my chair. Boulders knocked in the flooded river. Snow hushed the wind. "It's a good night for a story," I said. Hoho McKenzie licked one paw, passed it over the top of her head, and washed the back of one ear.

"I could a tale unfold– " she began.

"I've got a story!" Wiki interrupted.

"I thought we might hear one from our visitor."

"Why should she just walk in and expect an audience? Who does she think she is, anyway?"

"She told us her name."

"What sort of a name is Hoho?" asked Wiki.

Harry Wakatipu was feeling safe now he was sure Hoho wasn't the devil. "What sort of a name is Victoria Catherine Margaret ni-Houlihan O'Shaughnessy Flaherty Flynn?" he asked. That was Wiki's full name, but we never called her by it.

Wiki and Hoho stared at each other. "What's going on?" I whispered in Biff Piddington's ear.

"Your solitary life in the bush," he explained, "has led to your not understanding females."

"I understand them all too well. That's why I ran away from my mother."

"Not quite what I meant," said Biff Piddington. "Wiki is a female of strong personality."

"Yes?"

"Hoho is another female of strong personality. They are not going to get on together, not under one roof."

"Us jokers get on," I said. "Look at you and me and Harry Wakatipu."

"That is precisely what I mean. Us jokers as you put it do get on. Well, on the whole we do." Biff Piddington paused and said, "Mark my words. One of them will have to go."

Wiki and Hoho glared and looked away from each other. Outside the storm was roaring, but I'd have to be up and away before first light in my never-ending battle with the deer. "We'll hear the rest of your story tomorrow night," I told Hoho. "In the meantime, welcome to the Hopuruahine hut."

I climbed into my bunk. Wiki whispered something in Harry Wakatipu's ear. He sniggered, one clumsy hoof over his mouth, and looked at Hoho. He looked again, and his mane stuck up stiff with jealousy because Hoho was curled in my chair, her tiny tongue licking at a tin of condensed milk I had given her. Biff was asleep, guarding the door. Falling snow hushed the storm. I would have slept well but for the pong of Harry Wakatipu in my sleeping bag.

I woke once, and Biff Piddington was putting more wood on the fire. Harry Wakatipu muttered something in his sleep. It sounded like "mungee mungee taipo". Wiki was lying on my feet. She had one eye on Hoho McKenzie in my chair.

I sighed. We had a boar pig, a dog, a pack-horse, and a cat at the Hopuruahine. It was what I had always wanted, one big happy family. I turned over and slept.

Chapter Eight
Rhabdomancy at the Hopuruahine Hut

I got back from an early morning shoot to find my big happy family arguing hammer and tongs. The storm last night had brought down a slip. The river was brown as cocoa.

"I've been telling him for years he should dig a well near the hut," Harry Wakatipu was saying. "But will he listen to a thing I say? Now there's no water for me to have a wash."

"The liar!" I thought. Harry Wakatipu never had a wash in his life.

"Why did you not you dig the well yourself?" asked Biff Piddington.

"Who asked for your opinion?" Harry Wakatipu said in his most disagreeable voice

"If you'd filled the bucket last night when I told you," Wiki joined in, "there'd be plenty of clean water for breakfast."

"How preposterous," said Biff Piddington, "to be without clean, fresh water at the Hopuruahine. The precipitation in this watershed is greater than that over the rest of the Vast Untrodden Ureweras put together."

"So what, Pig?" Harry Wakatipu snarled. "Anyway,"

he said, "I don't need water for my breakfast. I can drink condensed milk."

"Who drank the last of the clean water last night because he was thirsty after swigging several tins of cond?" asked Wiki.

The dangerous Hopuruahine ford above the Cascades had been high so I was still wet-through. I drained my boots into a billy, tipped in the water out of my rifle barrel, and wrung out my swanny. There was just enough for a brew. I listened at the door again.

"If only somebody would dig that well, this wouldn't happen!" Harry Wakatipu repeated.

"Dig it yourself, Donkey!"

"Don't call me Donkey, Swine!"

"All right then, Ass!"

"Fill the bucket, Harry Wakatipu," said Wiki. "Fill it, and leave it to settle. Why you never do a hand's turn around the hut is beyond me."

"Shut up, Mongrel!"

"Who are you telling to shut up? Mule!"

They were still in bed, waiting for me to come home and light the fire. Biff Piddington and Wiki were getting as bone-idle as Harry Wakatipu.

Someone threw the bucket at someone else. There was another clang as they threw it back and missed. The bucket came sailing out the door. I caught it and walked inside in silence.

I got the fire going, and swung the billy for a brew while the stew heated in the camp oven. Wiki and Biff Piddington lay quiet. Harry Wakatipu sprawled on his bunk humming "You Are My Sunshine". He didn't know what it meant to be embarrassed.

Hoho McKenzie, alias Gladys Tuhakaraina, sat up in my chair, licked herself all over, yawned, and said, "I'll find you a spring."

"What a cheek!" said Harry Wakatipu.

"Who asked you to shove in your oar?" said Wiki.

"Water divination!" said Biff Piddington. "No better than palmistry and reading teacups. Next thing you'll be casting horoscopes."

I trimmed a wineberry branch to a fork, and gave it to Hoho McKenzie. "Show me where there's a spring, and I'll be eternally grateful."

Outside Hoho held the stick by the fork ends. The other end was vertical. "I can feel water," she said.

"And you can hear water," said Wiki. "The Hopuruahine River."

"It's pulling this way." The forked stick bent, pointing to the ground. Hoho tried to hold it up. The fork wrenched itself out of her hands and bounced on the ground.

"By Jove!" said Biff Piddington. Hoho's hands were bleeding, and the bark had been twisted off the stick. I stared. Wiki who was jealous of Hoho couldn't think of anything to say.

"Dig there," said Hoho.

Wiki took up the Y-shaped stick and held it the same way. Nothing happened. Biff Piddington took it in his powerful grip. It didn't work for him, either. Harry Wakatipu lounged out the door and snatched the stick rudely.

"Haw, haw!" he guffawed. "Harry Wakatipu, Water

Dowser!" He took a step, the stick twisted itself, and he clutched it tighter. The stick bent itself towards the ground. Harry Wakatipu cried, "I hate this stick!" It bent down, dragging him with it. "Make it let me go!" Harry Wakatipu shouted. The stick bent itself so hard it snapped in half. The end stuck in the ground, just where Hoho had said, and water bubbled clear. Harry Wakatipu had to have first taste and said it was very good.

"I do not believe what I have just observed," said Biff Piddington. "There must be some rational explanation."

"I wouldn't drink that water," said Wiki, "till it's been tested for poison." She looked at Hoho. "In any case I've often noticed it's damp there."

It tasted as good as the spring by my fly-camp on top of Manuoha, as good as the spring on top of the island on top of Lake Waikareiti, and there's no better water than that. Above Te Wai-iti, below Papatotara Saddle, there's a spring comes out of the side of the road. There's another one this side of the Mimiha, and another fine spring by Tamati Cairns's old hut, below Ohaua. They've all got the same sparkly, tasty water. Later, Hoho told me those springs had all been found by water diviners.

We boiled the billy, and I asked Hoho where she had learned dowsing.

"I come from a long line of Rhabdomancers," said the black cat with green eyes.

"Rhabdomancy?" said Wiki. It was clear she was jealous of Hoho.

"There's no such word," guffawed Harry Wakatipu. He was furious that she'd taken my chair ahead of him.

Biff nodded. "Rhabdomancy. A splendid word." He

60

was jealous of Hoho, too, but he loved long words, Biff Piddington. "Rhabdos, from the Greek word meaning a rod," he said. "Mancy – meaning divination by. The rod with which Hoho McKenzie, alias Gladys Tuhakaraina, divined water at the door of the Hopuruahine hut. Rhabdomancy!"

His bristly black face took a reddish shine. His little eyes went blood-shot. Even his tufted tail and the crest of bristles along his back blushed red. "Cat," he said, "I apologise. I permitted myself to indulge feelings of hostility, but you have demonstrated your right to a place in front of the fire. You are a veritable Rhabdomancer!"

It was a fine apology, if a little pompous. Wiki remained standoffish.

Harry Wakatipu brayed, "I wouldn't drink tea made from that spring. That's where everyone throws the washing-up water. And they do worse things, too." He grinned knowingly.

"You have already drunk from it," I reminded him. "From now on," I said, "nobody is to empty the basin out the door. And Harry Wakatipu, when you get up to have a piddle during the night, make sure you go well away from the hut. We don't want your pee in our tea."

"What about the Bogey-Man?" he whinged.

"If we can go to the dunny at night, so can you," said Wiki. I hoped her words meant she was going to welcome Hoho to the Hopuruahine, but Wiki was jealous as ever. She just didn't want Harry Wakatipu piddling in our spring.

"Hoho," I said, "last night you were about to tell us your story."

She arched her back as she sat in my chair and said, "I could a tale unfold– "

"You'll just have to keep it folded a while longer!" Wiki shoved past Hoho and lifted the lid off the camp oven. "The whole day's been wasted with all this ridiculous rhabdomancing. It's time for our tucker. We can have a story afterwards. I've got a good one about an old water dowser who lived by the Poplars in the Horomanga River."

Hoho's eyes flashed green, but she didn't seem to mind too much. We filled our plates with stew and sat around the hut, and there was the usual noise of feeding. Harry Wakatipu is a particularly rowdy swallower. I did hope we'd hear Hoho's story. She'd tried to tell it twice now and had been stopped by Wiki each time.

Chapter Nine
Storytelling at the Hopuruahine

"That was a good feed," Hoho sighed. "Do you eat like this all the time?"

"We eat our own weight in meat every few days." Wiki spoke fast. "We eat kiwis and huias and kakapos and kokakos and moas and– "

"They're all protected birds!"

"Not from us," said Wiki. "We eat slaters and weevils and slugs and snails– "

"You might," said Harry Wakatipu, "but I am a delicate eater."

"You'd live on condensed milk if you had your way!" Wiki looked angrily at him but jabbered fast, trying to hold the floor and stop Hoho from telling her story. Harry Wakatipu didn't know what was going on. He saw Wiki was furious but didn't understand what he'd done wrong, so he flapped his big lips and sneered. "Heh, heh, heh."

"I could a tale unfold– " Hoho began for the third time, but Wiki raised her voice higher.

"We eat sheep and cows and horses," she said.

"Nobody eats horses!" Harry Wakatipu squeaked.

"Do you mean to say you've never heard of the

dreaded Horse Cannibal?"

Harry Wakatipu shivered. "I don't think I want to hear this story," he said.

I knew Wiki was quick, but Hoho was quick, too. It was going to be interesting watching them competing for who was the best storyteller in the Hopuruahine hut.

"I'll tell a story," said Harry Wakatipu. He had beaten them both. Wiki and Hoho were so astonished they sat with their mouths open.

"My story is about a noble pack-horse." Harry Wakatipu spoke in his most affected manner. Biff Piddington shifted and said, "Get on with it."

"It is an epic story, mine," said Harry Wakatipu, "about Mr H. Wakatipu, pack-horse extraordinaire! I packed the corrugated iron, I carried the nails, I bore the tools, the axe, the cross-cut saw, the hammer, the maul, and the wedges which made the Hopuruahine hut. I found my way through the bush to Lake Waikaremoana. I blazed the track. I packed the tucker. I built the hut. I lit the fire. I boiled the billy. I made the tea. I cooked the tucker. I kept the deer culler company. I made sure he never got lost. I never answered back. I never pinched his chair nor nicked his bunk. I filled in the Daybook and the FS4s. I mapped the rivers and the mountains. I named the Hopuruahine, the Mokau, the Aniwaniwa, Manuoha, Maungapohatu, and Panekiri Bluffs. I baked the bread. I dug the dunny hole. I chopped the wood and split the kindling. I discovered Silver Pine Clearing up the Hopuruahine, the tarns on Manuoha, the way to the Tundra, and the saddle into the Ruakituri. I," said the lying old pack-horse, "I am H. Wakatipu which means: He Who Goes Before!"

Harry Wakatipu nodded and smiled around the hut. He clapped himself enthusiastically and bowed several times. "Thank you!" he said. "You are too kind. Thank you. Thank you."

"That's your story, is it?" I asked him.

"I packed the corrugated iron, I carried the nails, I bore the tools, the axe, the cross-cut saw, the hammer, the maul, the wedges which made the Hopuruahine hut." He was beginning it all over again. "I found my way through the bush to Lake Waikaremoana," he said. "I blazed the track. I packed the tucker. I built the hut. I– "

"Shut up!" we shouted together.

Harry Wakatipu's voice tailed away. "That's not how you tell a story," said Wiki. "Nobody's interested in anything you have to say, Harry Wakatipu."

"The horse," Biff Piddington explained to Hoho McKenzie, "cannot even light a fire. He will not deign to carry a pack. He neither chops firewood nor fetches water. He is a machine for the ingesting and digesting of condensed milk."

"What Biff means is Harry Wakatipu's a garbage-guts," Wiki said. Hoho sat up in my chair. She opened her mouth. The tip of her tongue appeared between her lips. She was just about to say, "I could a tale unfold..." again but Wiki beat her.

"This is the story of the ghostly go-ashore under the floor of the Hopuruahine hut," she said.

"I like a good ghost story," said Harry Wakatipu. "What's a go-ashore?"

"An iron pot with three legs," Biff Piddington told

him. "They brought them ashore off the sailing ships a century ago, so they were called go-ashores."

"Perhaps you'd like to tell this story?" Wiki asked.

Biff Piddington dropped his head back on my foot. He couldn't help answering questions. It was his training as a teacher.

"Once upon a time," said Wiki, "a deer culler crawled underneath the Hopuruahine hut and found something there in the dark, large, round, and made of iron. He knocked it with the handle of his skinning knife, and it rang like a bell. He tied on a rope.

"He pulled and pulled, but it wouldn't move. A couple of other deer cullers called at the hut, and they all pulled and pulled but it wouldn't move.

"The field officer rode over from Ruatahuna. He and his hack got on the end of the rope. They all pulled and pulled, but it wouldn't move.

"A couple of possum trappers called in. The two trappers and their dogs got on the end of the rope behind the deer cullers, the field officer and his horse, and they all pulled and pulled, but it wouldn't move.

"A party of three surveyors and their chainmen called in. They got on the end of the rope behind the deer cullers, the field officer and his horse, the two possum trappers and their pig dogs, and they all pulled and pulled, but it wouldn't move."

Each time some more people arrived in Wiki's story, Hoho McKenzie yawned. The first time she put her hand over her mouth. The second time she didn't bother. The third time she yawned rudely.

A bunch of four Wildlife rangers called in at the

66

Hopuruahine hut with their Labrador dogs," said Wiki. "They got on the end of the rope behind the deer cullers, their field officer and his horse, the two possum trappers and their pig dogs, the three surveyors and their chainmen, and they all pulled and pulled, but it wouldn't move."

"Ho, hum," groaned Hoho.

Wiki glanced at her. Harry Wakatipu's ears were sticking up. "Go on!" he said to Wiki.

"Five post splitters heading to the Aniwaniwa called in at the Hopuruahine hut to stay the night. They got on the end of the rope behind– "

"Behind the deer cullers, their field officer and his horse, the two possum trappers and their pig dogs, the three surveyors and their chainmen, and the four Wildlife rangers with their Labrador dogs, and they all pulled and pulled!" said Harry Wakatipu.

Wiki smiled. "But it wouldn't move!" she and Harry Wakatipu chanted together. Wiki nodded and Harry Wakatipu grinned back. He loves babyish stories where he's allowed to take part.

"A gang of six shearers called in at the Hopuruahine hut on their way to Galatea Station," said Wiki, "and– "

"And they got on the end of the rope behind the deer cullers, their field officer and his horse, the two possum trappers and their pig dogs, the three surveyors and their chainmen, the four Wildlife rangers and their Labrador dogs, and the five post splitters, and they all pulled and pulled!" said Harry Wakatipu. "And," he said. "And… And…"

"And it– " Wiki said, nodding.

"And it wouldn't move!" shouted Harry Wakatipu.

Hoho McKenzie lay on her back in my chair, her four feet in the air, and snored. I could hear the little bubbling grunt Biff Piddington makes when he's snoring, too.

"It sounds to me as if we'd better hear the rest of this story tomorrow night," I said. At once, Hoho's snoring stopped. She was wide awake, just waiting the chance to unfold her own story.

"A string of seven swaggers called in at the Hopuruahine hut," Wiki said at once.

"And they got on the end of the rope behind the deer cullers, their field officer and his horse, the two possum trappers and their pig dogs, the three surveyors and their chainmen, the four Wildlife rangers and their Labrador dogs, and the five post splitters, and the gang of six shearers," said Harry Wakatipu excitedly. "And they all pulled and pulled, and it wouldn't move!" He looked at Wiki. "Go on!" he said.

Hoho snored steadily. Biff Piddington laid down across the door. Wiki's eyes drooped. I climbed into my bunk. Harry Wakatipu was still trying to get Wiki to go on with the story. It was no use. Hoho had lost again. Wiki was a bit too much of a storyteller for her. I smiled to myself. I could hear Harry Wakatipu saying, " –and their pig dogs, the three surveyors and their chainmen, and the four Wildlife rangers and their Labrador dogs, and…" as I drifted off to sleep.

I woke. It was time to go for a shot. I threw my tea billy and a few rations in my pikau. It was dark inside the hut. I'd have liked to ask Wiki to go with me for company but she was fast asleep. Harry Wakatipu was lying on his bunk, mumbling something in his sleep about seventy-five stockbuyers and their kelpie dogs, and seventy-six mounted policemen and their bull-mastiffs. I had to step over Biff Piddington to get outside.

It was raining, and hailing, and turning to sleet, an ordinary morning at the Hopuruahine. I'd get across the ford before the snow started. By the time I got to where the Orangihikoia comes down into the Orangitutaetutu, it should be light. If I got a deer, I'd boil the billy and grill the kidneys for breakfast. I picked up my rifle, and a voice asked, "Where are you going?"

"For a shot."

Hoho came out from under the hut. There was dirt on her nose and whiskers, as if she had been digging. She slung my pikau on her back.

"I'll carry your pack," she said. "I'll keep you company and see you don't get lost in the Vast Untrodden Ureweras."

I strode up the track. Hoho McKenzie bounded over the logs and boulders. She stopped once and arranged the billy so it didn't make a clatter and warn the deer. She was going to make a good mate.

Chapter Ten
Hunting with Hoho

The deer that morning were fed-up with the rain. They stood in the open, ears, tails hanging down. The sky was so low I had to crouch. When it's like that you can poke holes in the clouds with your fingers, only it lets more rain through.

I had to swim the dangerous ford at the top of the Cascades. Hoho crossed somehow without getting her fur wet. After a few hours I stopped where the Orangihikoia joins the Orangitutaetutu, leaned my rifle against the big beech tree, and went to light a fire. Hoho had it going already and was grilling kidneys on a stick . She had a good hand for making things comfortable. The flames reflected red off the low clouds. Daylight was coming up.

I squatted beside Hoho and melted the ice off my beard. The water in the billy steamed and turned itself over the way it does just before boiling. The tea Hoho made was good and strong. It ran hot all the way down inside until I could feel it filling up my toes, my feet and legs. I drank another mug and felt it trickling down both arms right out to the insides of my fingertips. My finger-nails turned brown with hot tea.

"Deer cullers turn brown as they get older," I told Hoho. "From crouching over smoky fires, smoking wet tobacco, and drinking tea. You can always tell an old deer culler by the colour of his blood."

I'd knocked the skin off one knee in the ford and stood on the end of a stick that leapt up and took the skin off the other knee. I took out my knife now, ran it on the steel, and nicked the back of my left hand, enough to make it bleed.

"What are you doing?"

"Bad luck always comes in threes," I said. "I'm making sure the third bit of bad luck is just this nick."

"You're superstitious," said Hoho. "Oh!" The back of my hand was bleeding brown.

"It's the tea coming out," I said. "Deer cullers get cut so often they lose most of the blood they start off with. If old deer cullers don't drink tea all the time, they dry up crisp as a dead leaf, and blow away in the first wind."

"Where do old deer cullers go when they die?" asked Hoho.

"In the middle of the Grim Inscrutable Ureweras there's a secret clearing called the Old Deer Culler's Cemetery. They know when their time's up. The secret clearing's heaped with their bones. There's stacks of their old Long Toms, worn-out skin bags, cracked camp ovens, billies with the bottoms burnt out, ground-down skinning knives, axes sharpened back to the handle, and mugs worn down on the side the old deer cullers drank from."

"It makes a good yarn," said Hoho. "I must tell that horse. He scares easy."

"You go easy on Harry Wakatipu," I told her. "He's a despicable coward."

We both grinned as Hoho put on the pikau again. I took up my rifle. I felt snug inside my swanny. Wool keeps you warm, the field officer says, even if it's wet through.

We climbed through the clouds and shot the bush up the Orangihikoia, stopping and boiling the billy every few days to warm up the insides of our fingers and toes with hot tea. We threw up bivvies of ponga fronds, sidled the faces under Whakataka, untangled the water-shed at the head of the Maunganuiohau, dropped down the Huiarau, and came out at the orchard on the far side of the Hopuruahine. It took several weeks, but a sugarbag of deer tails floated behind me as I swam the river to the hut. Hoho paddled herself across dry on a bit of totara bark.

The ashes in the fireplace were cold and wet from snow sifting down the chimney. Harry Wakatipu was in his sleeping bag. Empty condensed milk tins stood on the noggins behind his bunk. They lay all over the floor.

"Where's Wiki?" I asked. "What's happened to Biff?"

A rangiora leaf was propped on the mantelpiece. On it were some ill-spelled words written in charcoal: "*Wee shal retrun   Whicky and Biph Pidingtunn*"

"You've driven my friends away again," I shouted at Harry Wakatipu. "I can't leave the hut for five minutes but you go upsetting everyone."

"You drove them away yourself," said Harry Wakatipu sidling towards the fire. I sat in my chair before he got into it.

"What do you mean?"

"It's only natural Wiki's upset. That cat wants to tell stories all the time. And Biff Piddington's upset because you took her fly-camping instead of him," said Harry Wakatipu. "Good riddance to bad rubbish I say."

I shivered and read the rangiora leaf again. "It says here they're coming back."

"I wouldn't count on that," sneered Harry Wakatipu.

Chapter Eleven

Wiki, Biff, and the Go-Ashore

Hoho heard Harry Wakatipu's cynical sneer. She found Wiki difficult, Biff Piddington a bit long-winded, but she really liked them both. I reminded myself we were all just one big happy family.

"Wiki and Biff have gone away," I told her. "But they're coming back."

Hoho took the rangiora leaf and read the message. "Can that pack-horse write?" she asked.

"I taught him how," I said, "but he can't spell. Why?"

"Who wrote this then?"

Harry Wakatipu sneered and flapped his big lips, "Heh, heh, heh!" He sounded less cocksure.

"Whose writing is this?" asked Hoho.

I looked at the message again. "*Wee shal retrun   Wicky and Biph Pidingtunn*"

"Wiki always uses full stops," I said.

"There's none here."

"Biff's a careful speller," I said.

"This was written by somebody who can't spell and can't punctuate," said Hoho. "The forger must be a liar as well as a poor speller, ignorant of punctuation, and a clumsy writer."

"Who could it be?" I looked around the Hopuruahine hut. "We've been away fly-camping, so we can't have written it. There's only you and me and…"

"And who else?"

"There's only you and me and…" I looked at the nasty old pack-horse who had somehow got into my chair. "And…and…" I mumbled.

Hoho licked one paw and washed the back of her neck. "So who do you think wrote the message?"

"Well it can't have been you, and it can't have been me, because we weren't here, so it must have been– "

"Why are you looking at me?" shouted Harry Wakatipu. "It's not fair. Pick on someone your own size!" He shouted louder. "It was all right here till that cat came, driving my friends away, sitting in my chair, stealing my condensed milk." He covered his face and blubbered, but the whites of his eyes flashed between his fingers.

"Why did you write that note?" I tipped him out of the chair on to the floor, his feet scrabbling sideways. "Where are they?"

Harry Wakatipu reared up on his hind legs like a boxing kangaroo. "I hate you all!" He jumped out the door and galloped down the flats.

"We must find Wiki and Biff," said Hoho.

"Let's have a brew of tea first."

"We must find them before it's too late." Hoho pricked up her ears. "I can hear a tiny voice screaming somewhere."

I listened but I'm deaf in my left ear because of the shooting.

"Perhaps you can dowse for them!" I ran and cut

another forked wineberry stick. Hoho held the thick end straight up, her thumbs over the forks to keep the magnetism from leaking, and walked towards the door. The dowsing rod bent straight down, twisting off the bark as it struggled and snapped itself in half. The broken piece jammed between two floorboards.

"Under the hut!"

We crawled and felt in the darkness. Between the totara blocks I'd built the hut upon, there was something huge and round. I donged it with my skinning knife, and it rang like a great bell.

"Remember Wiki's story about the go-ashore under the Hopuruahine hut?" asked Hoho.

"That was just a story."

"Does that sound like a story?" She pushed my ear against the shadowy bulge of the iron go-ashore. It was like listening to a railway line for the train. So far away it sounded half-smothered, a pig grunted. I listened again and thought I heard a distant dog's bark.

"They're running out of air!" said Hoho. I dug, and she scratched. Ancient carved planks, hand-made nails, old-fashioned egg-shaped whisky bottles, bones, knife handles, musket barrels, cartridge cases, a spade guinea, barrel staves, cannon balls flew out with the dirt. I could feel the rim of the go-ashore.

My hands broke through into space. I made the hole bigger so fresh air could get under. Hoho put her head into the hole and called. "Wiki! Biff!" There was no reply.

Hoho took a deep breath and squeezed through the hole. A few minutes, and a white-tipped tail stuck out. I pulled, and Wiki came out backwards. She was breathing but her eyes were closed. I made the hole bigger and dragged out Biff. Hoho scrambled out coughing, gulping the fresh air, and brought the bucket, splashing water over Wiki's face, holding it up for Biff to drink.

"For that relief, much thanks!" Biff's face which had been white was returning to its usual healthy black. We closed Wiki's mouth and blew in her nostrils. Her chest stirred. Hoho blew in her nose again, gently. Wiki's chest rose. She struggled and began breathing for herself.

"You're both alive!" I wiped big tears off my cheeks. They were sweat. A deer culler never cries.

We got Wiki and Biff inside. Hoho boiled the billy and poured tea down their throats. She heated the stew and spooned it into their mouths.

Biff's throat was sore from calling out. "I could hear you," he said, "but could not make you hear me. The little dog barked until she fell unconscious."

"Poor Wiki," said Hoho. She pulled my sleeping bag over Wiki and laid her on my chair in front of the fire. That night they told us their terrible story.

"You know the story of the Ghostly Go-Ashore and how the deer culler and all the others tried to pull it out from under the Hopuruahine hut?" asked Wiki. Hoho and I nodded.

"Well, after you'd gone fly-camping, Biff Piddington and I lay in our sleeping bags and thought we couldn't be bothered getting up. Harry Wakatipu ordered us to light the fire, and we told him to light it himself. Then he said he wanted a mug of tea and something to eat, and we said we wanted a mug of tea and something to eat. Then he made a noise like a tap running, trying to make us get up and have a piddle. Once we were up, he hoped we'd light the fire."

"He always does that," I said.

Wiki grinned. "He sounded so like a tap he had to get up and have a piddle himself. We told him to light the fire since he was up, but he sat in your chair and moaned about how cold he was until I got sick of the sound and got up and lit the fire, and Biff cooked breakfast.

"Harry Wakatipu ate just about everything and hid so he wouldn't have to do the dishes. I thought he was in the dunny. That's where he usually goes. But he'd crawled under the hut. He might have climbed under to see if the go-ashore was really there. Of course, it wasn't true. I'd just made it up for that story the night before."

"Of course," I said. "How did it get there?"

"That's the interesting thing," said Wiki. "Harry Wakatipu yelled that he'd found the go-ashore and for us to bring a rope. When Biff and I saw the size of it, we knew we couldn't pull it out with a rope, not even if we had three deer cullers, and a field officer, and his horse, and– "

"Yes, yes. So what did you do?"

"You didn't say you erected the hut on top of a huge, iron pot," said Biff Piddington.

"I levelled the site with the shovel, dug holes for the totara blocks, and built the hut on top of them. If there'd been a huge, iron pot I'd have seen it."

"Aha!" Hoho combed her whiskers with her claws. Her eyes were just two green lines.

"What happened?" I asked.

"Wiki and I climbed inside the pot to see what was there," said Biff, "and it turned over on top of us. Clop!"

"Somebody had set it waiting like an iron trap," said Wiki. "We banged and shouted, but Harry Wakatipu didn't answer. Biff tried to dig a hole with his tusk so we could get some air. It got hotter and hotter. I couldn't breathe. My throat closed up. I couldn't scream. That's when I passed out."

"I, too, was rendered unconscious by the foul air," said Biff Piddington. "My last thought was that you would come to our rescue."

"You're very trusting, Biff."

"I have always reposed the greatest confidence in you both. That we are now safe and fully recovered from our ordeal is justification for that confidence." Hoho slanted her green eyes and looked at Biff. He sounded pompous, but that was just his way. Biff Piddington was a thoroughly decent pig when you got to know him.

"We must find Harry Wakatipu," said Wiki, "and tell him we're all right."

"Agreed," said Biff Piddington. "It is not his fault he is a donkey at times of crisis."

Harry Wakatipu must have been standing outside, ear pressed against the wall. He cantered inside the hut and flung his arms about them both. "I'm so pleased to see you back!" he brayed.

In no time Harry Wakatipu believed he had saved Wiki and Biff from dying under the great iron pot. He even began to tell us how he had dug them both out, breathed life into their unconscious bodies, and nursed them back to health.

"Thanks to H. Wakatipu, M.D!" he said.

"What do you mean?" asked Hoho.

"M.D. stands for Doctor of Medicine," said Harry Wakatipu. "I am a great doctor, but so modest I don't like to talk about how good I am."

"M.D. also stands for Muddled Donkey," said Biff Piddington. "However all's well that ends well."

I looked about the Hopuruahine hut and smiled. We were one big happy family again. "Tomorrow," I said, "Hoho will tell us her story."

"Not that dreary 'I could a tale unfold' again," said Wiki.

"Hoho just saved your life," I said. "You could show a little more gratitude."

"Thanks, Hoho," Wiki said.

"I, too, owe you a debt of eternal gratitude," said Biff Piddington. He sounded pompous but more convincing than Wiki.

There's just one thing I don't understand. I've got to say it, otherwise I wouldn't be telling the truth. But the truth is that I climbed under the hut, later, to have a look at the huge, iron pot that Hoho called a go-ashore, and there was nothing there. I couldn't even see where we'd shifted all that dirt to rescue Wiki and Biff. I said nothing to the others but looked forward to hearing Hoho's story that night. Perhaps it would explain something about the mysterious go-ashore under the Hopuruahine hut.

Chapter Twelve

The Horse Cannibal and the Cooking Pot

Next morning I looked under the hut, and the go-ashore sat there, dark and mysterious. I couldn't understand it.

"Shove these poles underneath," Hoho said, "and skid it out." She greased the skids with rancid butter. We shoved them under the huge, iron pot. Ponderous it slid into the light.

The go-ashore had three legs so a fire could be lit underneath. On one side a life-sized horse was engraved. Harry Wakatipu said it looked very like his father. Already he had forgotten his cowardice, as well as Wiki's and Biff Piddington's near-death. Harry Wakatipu is not the most sensitive of people.

I felt uneasy about the giant pot. It certainly hadn't been there when I built the Hopuruahine hut. It had vanished after we got out Wiki and Biff. Yet it sat there now, curved and sinister. Harry Wakatipu was delighted by what he called his father's picture and kept rubbing and polishing it. Biff sniffed and tapped the go-ashore with his one tusk. He seemed worried about something. I said nothing about the way the go-ashore kept appearing and disappearing.

The afternoon got darker. Even Harry Wakatipu stopped going near the huge iron pot. Wiki looked out the door at it, a snarl on her face. I told Biff I wasn't going for an evening shot. By the time I got down the flats it would be too late to see my sights. He shook his head.

Night came early. The go-ashore crouched grim. We built up the fire and tried to get warm, but icicles formed on the wall nearest the pot. We shivered despite the fire.

We were one big happy family, I told myself, but it didn't seem to help. Hoho McKenzie sat in my chair, and washed behind her ears. "I wish you wouldn't do that," said Wiki. "It makes it rain."

"It rained long before I came to the Hopuruahine."

"How do you know?"

"My great-grandfather lived at the Hopuruahine in the olden days," said Hoho, "and he told me a thing or two. Lake Waikaremoana was much bigger then. It took in Lake Taupo, and Lake Wairarapa, and Lake Manapouri. There were grassy flats the whole way round. Happy horses galloped on the grass and lived in houses thatched out of grass. They ate grass and drank from the lake."

"Why didn't they drink condensed milk?" asked Harry Wakatipu.

"It hadn't been invented."

"This story's stupid," said the rude pack-horse.

"There was one place the horses kept away from," Hoho went on. "The Hopuruahine!"

"Why?" asked Wiki. She didn't like Hoho telling a story but couldn't stop herself listening.

"For many years the horses' children kept disappearing from the Hopuruahine. The parents banned swimming in the lake, but still the young horses disappeared.

"The parents told their children to keep out of the the bush in case they got lost, but still the young horses disappeared. The parents told them to keep out of the cave behind the Mokau waterfall, but the young horses kept disappearing."

His mouth hanging open, Harry Wakatipu stared at Hoho McKenzie.

"The grown-up horses said, 'Stick to the grass around the lake. You can't go wrong if you keep on the grass,' they told their foals." Hoho nodded, and Harry Wakatipu's big head nodded up and down with hers.

"What happened?"

"The young horses kept on the grass," said Hoho, "but they still disappeared. Their mothers and fathers were in despair."

"I know!" shouted Harry Wakatipu. "Let's stop listening to this story, and have a tin of condensed milk."

"Shut up," said Wiki. "Go on, Hoho."

"One day," said Hoho, "my great-grandfather saw smoke rising where this hut now stands. He climbed a little rata vine and looked down here. And what do you suppose he saw?"

"Me!" shouted Harry Wakatipu. He likes to hear his name in stories.

"He saw a huge iron pot standing on three legs over a fire," said Hoho. "An ogre ran up from the grassy flats carrying half a dozen young horses. He threw them into the iron pot, cooked, and ate them."

"Oh!" Harry Wakatipu groaned.

"The ogre was a Horse Cannibal. Terrified my great-grandfather stuck a claw into the little rata vine and didn't move in case the Horse Cannibal looked up. That tiny rata grew into the huge tree up behind the Hopuruahine hut today."

"The hollow one?" asked Wiki.

"That's it. The little hole made by my great-grandfather's claw grew into the hollow."

"I'll swing the billy, and we'll have a brew of tea with lots of condensed milk and sing a happy song." Harry Wakatipu shivered and looked over his shoulder at the dark go-ashore.

"I want to hear what happened," said Wiki.

"I'm sure everybody's had enough of this story," Harry Wakatipu said with a ghastly grin.

"Suffer the Cat to finish her narrative," ordered Biff Piddington.

"My great-grandfather crept away and told the horses what he had seen. They searched the grassy Hopuruahine flats and found traps dug everywhere. Their children had kept on the grass, as they were told. They fell into the traps, and the Horse Cannibal ate them.

"The horses dug a trap several thousand feet deep at the mouth of the Hopuruahine. They covered it with grass, and baited it with a very fat horse, a criminal they fed on condensed milk."

"I'm not fat!" said Harry Wakatipu.

"The Horse Cannibal fell into the trap and broke his neck. The horses filled the hole and built a hill on top of it. You can see it down the flats today, that little hill sticking out on its own."

"What about the cooking pot?"

"They buried it. Nobody thought the deer culler would come along and build the Hopuruahine hut on top of it."

"It was the best site for a hut," I said. "It's flat. It gets the sun. There's firewood and water handy."

"Long before the deer culling began," said Hoho, "there were Maori huts here at the Hopuruahine. And long before Maori huts there were Horse huts. And long before Horse huts there was the Horse Cannibal's hut. There's been some sort of hut here for thousands of years. Before the Age of Horses there was the Age of Dogs when Dogs built huts at the Hopuruahine. And before the Age of Dogs, there was the Age of Cats. That's when my ancestors built huts and lived here."

"When I cleared the grass," I said, "there were lots of bones."

"Young horses eaten by the Horse Cannibal," said Hoho.

Harry Wakatipu climbed on to his bunk. "If I go to sleep," he said, "you won't blow out the candle, will you?"

Outside, the huge cooking pot of the Horse Cannibal shone black in the moonlight. It looked bigger than ever. Something was ringing.

"Come in and close the door," said Wiki. "I don't think anyone had better go near that pot tonight."

"I've got to go to the dunny," Harry Wakatipu whined.

"Can't you wait till morning?"

"I've got to go now."

Although the moon was bright I took my rifle and a candle in a tin. Biff Piddington stood at the door, a candle in one hand, the axe in the other. Wiki and Hoho waited inside with lumps of firewood.

Harry Wakatipu took ages. At last he finished. First he wanted me to walk in front, then he wanted me to walk behind. We flattened ourselves against the wall so we didn't have to go too close to that huge iron pot which seemed to have moved closer. Perhaps it was just the echo of the river that made it ring. I was glad to jump in the door and put the padlock on the heavy chain.

That's when Wiki said she had to go the dunny. Then it was Hoho. At last, Biff Piddington said he thought perhaps he had better go to the dunny, too. I'd just got him inside when I realised I'd have to go myself. "You're all being very childish," I said. "I can go by myself."

I was running back down the track, whistling *God Defend New Zealand*, when something grabbed my ankle. I screamed. Biff appeared with the axe, Wiki with a lump of firewood, and Hoho with the slasher. Around my ankle was the bush lawyer that had tripped me. We laughed, held hands, and ran past the huge, iron pot.

"You left me alone!" Harry Wakatipu screamed. "You left me as bait for the Horse Cannibal. I hate you all!"

We quietened him with a tin of condensed milk, had a last brew of tea, and climbed into our sleeping bags. And a little voice said, "I've got to go again."

"Harry Wakatipu," I said, "you don't."

"I've got to."

"Are you sure?"

"Well– no. But what if I have to get up in the night?"

"You'll just have to use the empty condensed milk tins under your bunk. If you wet the floor you can scrub

88

out the hut in the morning." I knew that would fix him.

Harry Wakatipu didn't get up again that night. He slept and snored. The Horse Cannibal didn't come smacking his lips and shaking the door. I know because all night I sat with my eyes on the door, lighting one candle from another.

It rained that day. The river flooded. We laid the buttered skids to the edge, slid the Horse Cannibal's cooking pot along them, and tipped it into the water where it floated black and menacing down the river. Out in the middle of Lake Waikaremoana the go-ashore tipped over and disappeared.

"The lake's bottomless," I told Harry Wakatipu. "The go-ashore will never worry us again."

"Come on!" he said. "First back to the hut wins a tin of condensed milk!" He's got longer legs but he didn't win because Wiki yelled, "Watch out for the Horse Cannibal!" That stopped him. He kept in the middle of us all the way back to the hut.

Where the go-ashore had sat outside the Hopuruahine hut, the ground still feels cold, even in summer. And in the middle of the lake there's a circle of black water nobody goes near. Other lakes start freezing from their edges in winter. Lake Waikaremoana always starts icing up from the middle where the Horse Cannibal's cooking pot sank.

I suppose I've got to tell you this to finish the story. Harry Wakatipu didn't get up and use the empty condensed milk tins that night. He wet his sleeping bag instead. Only it wasn't his sleeping bag. It was mine. He's a thorough-going nuisance, Harry Wakatipu.

Chapter Thirteen
Harry Wakatipu Behaves Badly

Each night Wiki and Hoho took it in turn to tell stories. Each morning Biff Piddington baked fresh bread. Each evening a stew bubbled and winked in the camp oven. The hut was scrubbed and swept clean. Wiki cut the firewood; Hoho kept the water bucket full; Biff slashed the track to the dunny so you didn't get wet pushing through the long grass. Life with my big, happy family was so good I didn't want to go hunting. It was more fun sitting around talking to Biff and listening to Wiki and Hoho.

My tail-line had nothing much on it, but that didn't matter. I'd go fly-camping and bring back a packful of deer tails before the field officer came again.

Biff Piddington looked at my FS4s for the last few weeks and said, "You must improve your tally."

"She'll be right," I told him. "We've earned a bit of a spell."

There never was such a summer at the Hopuruahine. We went on picnics around the lake. We swam, caught trout and eels, rolled them in newspaper and cooked them in the ashes. Or we cooked them in hangis. The deer thought it was Christmas and fed out on the clearings during the day. Only one person wasn't happy.

Hoho had stolen his chair; Biff Piddington was drinking his condensed milk; Wiki wouldn't tell him his special bedtime story every night. Harry Wakatipu grouched all that lovely summer.

"There's only half a case of condensed milk left."

"You're the one who guzzled it," I told him, "and it's my condensed milk, not yours. It might be an idea if you cut out the complaining and did a bit of work occasionally."

"It might be an idea if you did a bit of fly-camping and shot a few deer occasionally," snarled Harry Wakatipu.

"That's it!" I took him by the ear and ran him outside. His behind was so fat from all the condensed milk he stuck in the door. I kicked, and he popped out like a cork. Wiki, Hoho, and Biff Piddington laughed.

"I'll get my revenge," swore Harry Wakatipu.

I threw him a piece of soap. "Get yourself a wash first. You stink!"

We all laughed again. A stone landed on the roof.

"Every stone on the roof means another night you can sleep out in the bush!" I shouted.

Another stone landed.

"And I hope the Horse Cannibal eats you!" I shouted.

There was a terrified whinny. No more stones landed on the roof.

"I wonder if that was wise," murmured Biff Piddington.

"What?"

"Scaring Harry Wakatipu with the Horse Cannibal."

"It stopped him."

"Nevertheless," said Biff Piddington, "may I suggest

you go fly-camping tomorrow and enlarge your tally of deer tails?"

"Tomorrow we're having a hangi at the waterfall," I said. "It's too hot hunting the bush this weather. The field officer knows that."

He didn't know that at all. Next day the others were swimming and diving under the waterfall, I was opening the hangi, and the field officer arrived. Harry Wakatipu had run all the way over the Huiarau Range to Ruatahuna and told on us.

The field officer looked at my empty tail line. "I'll be back in a few months," he said, "and you'd better have a decent tally. And what's the idea, giving poor old Harry Wakatipu such a hard time?" I stared open-mouthed. Deer cullers aren't allowed to answer back.

"As for you lot," he said to Wiki, Biff Piddington, and Hoho. "You'd better clear off and let him get on with his work or he'll be down the road."

It was lucky the hut was clean, and there was lots of firewood, fresh bread, and a stew for the field officer's tea. He might have given me the bullet if the place had been in a mess. The only thing untidy and smelly was Harry Wakatipu's bunk, so I had to sleep on that. The field officer slept on mine.

"You're welcome to ride out on my pack-horses," the field officer said to Wiki, Hoho, and Biff, "as far as Ruatahuna." I remembered how lonely he was. That's why he used to ride over to hear Wiki's stories on a Saturday night. Now he'd have two storytellers of his own. And he'd keep Biff Piddington to count his stores and fill in his reports. The field officer couldn't add. He couldn't read very well. And his writing was poor.

"You'll have to pad the hooks with a sack or your behinds'll get pretty sore," he said. "You can use the pack-straps as stirrups, but don't blame me if your foot slips through and you get dragged." He didn't mean to be gruff, but that's how it sounded.

The field officer swung up into his saddle. "Recite Rule Three of the Deer Culler's Daybook," he ordered.

I repeated the terrible words: "A deer culler has no friend but loneliness, no companion but his rifle, no home but his sleeping bag."

"And you'd better not forget it!" said the field officer.

Wiki, Hoho, and Biff seemed excited as they rode up the track. They didn't even turn and wave.

"No friend but loneliness." I swung up my pack and sidled Wairere Bluffs. I'd cut across the Mokau to the Tundra and fly-camp the Ruakituri for six months. It felt quite good in the bush on my own again.

"No companion but my rifle." I gazed up the blue ridges like giant steps into the sky. I looked below at Lake Waikaremoana stretching its great unbroken curve to where you fell over the edge if you rowed the dinghy too far.

"No home but my sleeping bag."

I'd padlocked the door, hidden the key in a new place. And in case Harry Wakatipu found a way in I'd left a dummy sitting on his bunk. In the gloom it looked like the Horse Cannibal. I was going to get my own back on Harry Wakatipu for breaking up my happy family. He had behaved very badly.

Chapter Fourteen

Harry Wakatipu and the Puppet

Harry Wakatipu climbed down the chimney and was scared silly by the dummy of the Horse Cannibal. I got back from the Ruakituri, loaded with deer tails, and he made up some cock and bull story about how I'd left my beautiful Hardy split-cane fly rod in the middle of the floor, and he'd tripped over it. I know he broke it deliberately, to get his own back. He has a nasty streak, Harry Wakatipu.

Next day the field officer arrived from Ruatahuna and destroyed my deer tails on a fire he lit with the bits of my broken rod. "Keep it up," he grunted and rode away. He liked to think he was a man of few words. I knew he kept Wiki and Hoho prisoners at the base-camp so they could tell him stories each night. And he made Biff Piddington read him my mother's letters that he never delivered, and the *Woman's Weekly* she sent me. I knew because every few months I got a message in a bottle down the Hopuruahine River. I knew everything going on at the base-camp.

A tall narrow oil bottle floated down the river one day. It contained a beautiful four-piece fly rod, one I could carry in my pack. "M. H. R!" said the note. "H. B.

from W., H., and B.P." I knew what the message meant but didn't dare say it aloud in case Harry Wakatipu heard and told on me. Deer cullers aren't allowed birthdays. Rule Three forbids it.

I was trying out my new rod when something else came bobbing and flashing out of the gorge below the Hopuruahine Cascades. It shone slick as it turned, rolling and glistening, black and sluggish, like a drowned man. I made a couple of false casts, dropped my fly on it, and played the dead weight with the tip of my rod, humouring it, backing across the shingle ever so slowly because my trace was a single hair pulled out of Harry Wakatipu's tail. I had on a No. 18 Wiki's Favourite and could see it like a gay pinhead against the dark thing slumped in the water. Not daring to use the reel I drew in the spare line with my left hand and took the weight on the tip again. The trace and the tiny hook held. The sinister thing grounded at my feet.

It was a tarred canvas bag with a message painted in white: "We shall return. Love from Wiki, Biff, Hoho."

That morning Harry Wakatipu had stuck out his tongue and answered back when I told him to light the fire. "I'll teach him," I said. If this present was something to eat, I'd scoff the lot myself. That's what Harry Wakatipu did, the time his mother sent him a cake. I'd been waiting a long time to get my own back.

I tipped out the bag in the hollow rata behind the hut. There were some clothes, some bits of wood, a round thing the size of a head, and a couple of carved wooden hands painted white. There was a hat, a pair of wooden feet, a pair of shoes. I put them together. It made a lifesize puppet with a white face and hands. The hat, clothes, and shoes were black. I was scared and pushed the puppet over with the butt of my rod. It didn't look so human lying on its side. I gave the canvas bag another shake. Out fell a book called, *Teach Yourself Ventriloquism.*

Ventriloquism I found was throwing your voice so it came from somewhere else. I practised till I could make my voice come out of a rock a couple of hundred yards away. An old stag was just going to strip the leaves off a broadleaf when I threw my voice into the tree.

"Don't eat me!" I said. The old stag farted and leapt backward. He looked around, in case someone had seen him making a fool of himself, and went to take a mouthful of leaves. "How would you like it if I bit you?" the tree asked him. The stag jerked up his head so hard both antlers fell off. He laid back his ears and ran away bawling. I was ready for Harry Wakatipu.

Around the corner from the Hopuruahine hut, there's the grave of a possum trapper who stirred a teaspoon of cyanide instead of sugar into his tea. I hid nearby one afternoon. Harry Wakatipu was stealing cherries over in the orchard. It was dark when he trotted home through the dusk, smacking his big lips, his puku bulging with cherries. I threw my voice so the grave groaned beside him, "Come here, Harry Wakatipu!"

I ran after him. I didn't want any dead possum trapper grabbing my foot and dragging me into the grave. In the hut the coward jumped on the top bunk and wouldn't come down for a couple of days.

Every time he went near the possum trapper's grave

after that, I threw my voice and made a groan come out of the ground. He didn't dare go near the orchard again. I scoffed all the cherries.

He was crossing the river one day when I threw my voice, like a crocodile gnashing its teeth.

"Who's that?" cried Harry Wakatipu.

"I love the taste of horse!" a crocodily voice croaked beside him. He refused to leave the hut for a couple of weeks after that.

"What's wrong?" I asked.

"Nothing," he said, but his eyes flashed white.

When he poked his nose outside again, I was waiting and threw my voice so it hissed like a giant snake. Harry Wakatipu leapt inside and slammed the door. I grinned and went off to shoot some deer.

I livened up Harry Wakatipu with a few other tricks and thought it was time he met the puppet. I'd been practising each day in the hollow rata and could work it pretty well.

I rigged the puppet so it lay back on my bunk. While I boiled the billy and had a brew of tea, the greedy pack-horse stole a tin of condensed milk and sneaked off to pinch my bunk. He smirked away to himself. He thought I was so dumb I hadn't noticed. As he lay down, I pulled a string, and the puppet sat up beside him. Its ghastly white face shone. Its black eyes gleamed. It pointed one white finger at Harry Wakatipu, and I threw my voice and pulled another string so it opened its mouth and said, "Thief!"

Harry Wakatipu went through the wall of the Hopuruahine hut. His iron shoes struck sparks as he galloped shrieking down the river-bed.

I left the puppet lying in my chair and tied its strings to the latch so it sat up and pointed when Harry Wakatipu tried to sneak in the door next morning. That kept him out of the hut for a week. I got pretty good at making the puppet slip down off the bunk and walk across the floor, but Harry Wakatipu grew used to it in the end. He never liked it though and drew his lips back off his teeth and spat whenever it moved.

"I hate that puppet!" he used to say.

I went fly camping for a few weeks. When I got back I went to light the fire and saw the tip of a wooden shoe in the ashes. I scrabbled through them and found a couple of wooden knuckles and half an ear.

"You burnt the puppet!" I said to Harry Wakatipu who was tiptoeing towards the door, but he galloped away. He sneaked in late that night. I was waiting and said, "You killed the puppet."

"He wasn't real," said Harry Wakatipu. "You just carved him out of a bit of kahikatea with your skinning knife."

"If he wasn't real, how did he talk?" Harry Wakatipu was silent.

"You killed him."

"He burned just like a bit of wood."

"You'd burn, too, if I put you on the fire." Harry Wakatipu was silent again. "I'm going to tell the police," I told him. "They hang you for murder."

Harry Wakatipu's scared of being hanged because he's got such a long neck. He took off, and I didn't see him for ages. One day I saw his tracks leading into the

99

cave across the river. I waited till after dark and threw my voice into the cave. "I am the ghost of the puppet!" I said, and Harry Wakatipu galloped out shrieking.

Then I lost my book on ventriloquism. I searched through the sacks and old swannies on the top bunk. I even looked under Harry Wakatipu's bunk but didn't like to crawl in there because of the pong. I couldn't find my book. Even worse, I forgot how to throw my voice.

Then some strange things happened. I was coming home past the possum trapper's grave in the dark when an awful groan came out of the ground. I ran all the way back down to the lake and climbed home around Tomorrow Ridge. I didn't get to the hut till six o'clock next morning.

Another time I was about to cross the river to the hut when I heard a crocodile clashing its teeth. I had to sleep on the other side. I could see Harry Wakatipu sitting in the hut, drinking my condensed milk, and burning all my firewood. I shouted for him to come and carry me across, but he pretended he couldn't hear.

Then I heard the crocodile crawling towards me, and a lion roared up in the bush. That's when I climbed a tree. Every time I went to climb down, the lion and the crocodile stamped around below, bellowing. Even worse, a snake hissed in the branches above me. I sat very still all night. It's lucky I don't scare easily.

When it got light, I dived from the tree into the river and swam across before the crocodile could catch me. Once inside the hut I was all right. I booted Harry Wakatipu out and told him that was the end of him sleeping in my bunk.

And then I carved another puppet in the shape of a dragon. Harry Wakatipu's scared stiff of dragons because he thinks they eat horses. I can't wait to see him come home and find the dragon lying on his bunk. I wish he'd hurry up and come home. It's not much fun on your own in the Hopuruahine hut with all the voices that seem to come out of the corners. Once there'd have been Wiki and Biff Piddington and Hoho McKenzie to keep me company, but that pack-horse got rid of them because he's jealous. It's typical of Harry Wakatipu to be late. He's got no sense of humour, and he never thinks of anyone but himself.

Chapter Fifteen
The Reflections of Harry Wakatipu

The dragon puppet scared the living daylights out of Harry Wakatipu. I warned him if he didn't sweep out all the empty condensed milk tins under his bunk the dragon would come back. As I left for a fly-camp up the right branch of the Hopuruahine, Harry Wakatipu was cleaning out the hut.

I got a few deer off the big slips, but would have got a lot more if I'd been able to find my field glasses. Before the Vast Untrodden Ureweras shrunk, it took several days to cross some of those slips, so it paid to glass them before firing a shot.

My ammo ran out, and I dropped down to the hut. There wasn't an empty condensed milk tin in sight. The only sign of Harry Wakatipu was his pong.

I scoured the camp oven with sand, in case he'd been using it for something disgusting, and got a loaf baking. A book by Flann O'Brien lay open on the table. I read the first words: "*If a man stands before a mirror and sees in it his reflection–* " and threw the book under Harry Wakatipu's bunk. Deer cullers aren't even allowed to think about looking in mirrors. It makes them soft.

I loaded my pack with ammo and bread. On a

rangiora leaf I wrote a message with a bullet. "You'd better have a look at Rule Three in the Daybook before you go reading any more of that filth about looking in mirrors."

I climbed up Dry Creek, worked the rest of the slips, and shifted to my camp on top of Manuoha. At evening I liked to sit up there and pick out Lake Waikaremoana miles below. Cloud would pour up the Waikaretaheke from Hawke Bay and spread over the lake till it looked like a star crashed amongst the ridges. One afternoon, as the sun was going down, I saw lights flashing down there and knew I was seeing things.

Blow me down if I didn't see those lights again next morning. They shone where the Hopuruahine flats would be, if you could see that far. "Real jokers don't let their imaginations run away with them," I told myself. "You'd better get down to the Hopuruahine hut. Take it easy a day or two."

Down at the hut I lay around eating big feeds. Harry Wakatipu didn't show up but the place ponged of him. He couldn't be far away.

One day I dropped over Tomorrow Ridge. I was going to sneak up the Hopuruahine flats to the hut, picking up a tame deer or two. But instead of deer, three-legged contrivances zigzagged in parallel rows the length of the flats. It looked as if all the surveyors in the country had set up their theodolites.

Harry Wakatipu's tracks were everywhere. The first tripod – split totara tied together with supplejack – held the top off a condensed milk tin.

"He's polished it bright with his tongue. Ha! Ha! Ha!"

The next tripod held exactly the same thing, the top cut off a condensed milk tin. And the next, and the next…

The sun winked off the parallel rows of polished tin lids. Those were the lights I'd seen from Manuoha. But what was it all for? I examined one more closely, the top off a condensed milk tin, as shiny as a mirror.

For one terrible moment I thought I'd seen my reflection in it. Rule Three of the Deer Cullers' Daybook says: "Any man caught looking at himself in a mirror will be sent down the road."

"Lucky I didn't see myself in that shiny tin," I said in case the field officer was watching through his field glasses. He'd read my lips and know I was innocent.

Next morning there was an overpowering stench of pack-horse, and I dragged Harry Wakatipu from under the hut. He stunk something terrible. "Go and scrub yourself in the river," I told him. He went willingly, as if wanting to please me.

I was frying a feed when he came back and stood so close he dripped into the camp oven. "Back off!" I said and looked at him. Overnight his bay coat had turned white.

That filthy book was the cause of the trouble, he admitted at last. "It's about how when you look in a mirror you see a yourself a bit younger," he said.

"What?"

"Read it!" He shivered and ponged like the coward he is. Out of pity for the gutless pack-horse, I took the book between my thumb and forefinger and read the whole of the first sentence.

"If a man stands before a mirror and sees in it his reflection, what he sees is not a true reproduction of himself but a picture of himself when he was a younger man."

You look in a mirror. That takes a bit of time. The mirror reflects your image. That takes another bit of time. You're actually seeing yourself as you were when you were a bit younger. "It's true!" I thought. "Set up enough mirrors reflecting each other, you'll see yourself when you were just born."

I looked at Harry Wakatipu. "Those tins," I asked, "down the flats, they're set up to reflect each other, aren't they?"

He nodded.

"You've been looking in them, haven't you?" He blushed. "But you couldn't see your reflection very many times, just looking into them," I said. And then I dropped to it. "All right, Harry Wakatipu, where are my field glasses?"

That's what got him talking. Real jokers are silent, laconic, and taciturn, but words gushed out of Harry Wakatipu like the Hopuruahine in flood. I was deeply embarrassed but listened because he was my pack-horse. I felt responsible for him.

He'd set up a few condensed milk tin tops so they reflected each other, and tried looking in them. "I could see myself looking younger each time I added another," he said. "I added more and more but couldn't see because the reflection got too small."

"So you swiped my field glasses?" He nodded. "Then what?"

"I cut the tops off all the old tins under my bunk. I

105

polished them with my tongue, stuck them up on tripods, and looked in them."

"It shows a lack of manliness," I told him. "I'll be surprised if the field officer keeps you on this time. What did you see?"

Harry Wakatipu had looked at his image reflected a thousand times, growing younger and younger till he was just a new-born foal. Then he flogged my field glasses and looked through them at his tin mirrors, going back through time. He saw his father growing younger and younger, then his grandfather, and so on back down a hundred generations of horses. Eyes nearly pulled out of their sockets by the thousands of years he was looking back, he saw his first ancestor.

That's what turned his hair white. Harry Wakatipu found himself staring into the eyes of the Horse Cannibal.

"I focused your field glasses to see him better," he snivelled. It's a sacking offence for a deer culler to cry, but I suppose you can't expect any better of a pack-horse.

"What did he look like?"

"He had big sharp teeth!"

"Pull yourself together, man!" I exclaimed.

"I'm a pack-horse," he wept. "The Horse Cannibal teeth were all filed to a point. And he was looking back at me!"

"He couldn't have."

"If I can look back through mirrors, somebody at the other end must be able to look forward. He beckoned to me to come to him, and he… he… "

"Yes? He what?"

"I don't want to say."

"Tell me."

"Don't make me say it!"

"What did the Horse Cannibal do?"

"He licked his lips! He's coming through all those tin mirrors to eat me!"

"I'm going down the flats to knock them over," I said. "Once they're gone, there'll be no way the Horse Cannibal can find you." I laced up my boots. "By the way," I said, "where are my field glasses."

"I dropped them when I saw the Horse Cannibal."

"You left my good field glasses out in all the weather! I ought to let him eat you."

I found them all right, my good field glasses. I was tempted to look at the first tin mirror, just as a scientific experiment. "Come on," I said aloud to myself, "push over the first tripod and it'll knock down the next, and so on, like a pack of cards." I went to do it but couldn't help having a quick look through the field glasses. As I did so a voice neighed, "What'd I tell you? He's looking at himself in those mirrors!"

It was Harry Wakatipu, and the field officer was with him. I kicked the first tripod. It knocked the next to the ground, and the next, and the next. A few minutes and the last one tumbled on the deer-nibbled grass.

"Were you looking at yourself?" The field officer put my field glasses to his eyes and tossed them back. "Better shout yourself a new pair." I looked through them myself and could see only a blur.

The field officer lit a fire, burned all my deer tails, and entered the number in his Area Book. "I don't know what you're up to," he said, climbing on his horse, "but you'd better cut it out."

As he rode away, I poked Harry Wakatipu out from under the hut. "You tried to get me sacked," I said. "You're banned from the Hopuruahine hut for life." I got in a few good clouts before he bolted. "I hope the Horse Cannibal eats you!" I shouted.

A few weeks later I went into Rotorua with the field officer and a string of pack-horses to pick up the gear for the next season. Ammunition, tents, camp ovens, axe handles, swannies, files, sacks of tobacco, rolls of number eight wire, and thousands of cases of condensed milk. While in Rotorua I bought a new pair of field glasses. The expert in the shop took one look through my old ones and shook his head. "What have you been doing with these?"

"Glassing deer."

"Don't you know you can strain field glasses?" said the man. "These have had it. You're not supposed to look too great a distance through them."

It was Harry Wakatipu looking back so far down the centuries to the Horse Cannibal, he'd worn out all the magnification, strained my good field glasses.

I bought a new pair, 8 X 36s, and the field officer grinned when I told him the old ones were strained. "Next thing you'll be telling me you've strained your rifle barrel, shooting too far," he said. "What are you? A girl?"

He was the field officer, so I couldn't answer back. Besides, I was supposed to be a man of few words. Rule Three in the Daybook says, "A deer culler is reticent,

laconic, and taciturn." It also says, "Any man caught looking at his reflection in a mirror, a shop window, or a
river will get the bullet, and his name will never be mentioned again in the Vast Untrodden Ureweras. N.B. It is
best if deer cullers are kept in ignorance about girls so
they can't go looking at any reflections in their eyes."

"What are girls?" I asked the field officer as we loaded
the pack-horses. That should make it clear I was a real
joker.

"Real jokers don't waste words," said the field officer,
and we rode in silence for several months across the
Kaingaroa Plains towards the Vast Inscrutable Ureweras.
I thought to myself next time I saw Harry Wakatipu I'd
tell him he was a mirror-kisser. That wouldn't be wasting words.

Chapter Sixteen

Harry Wakatipu and
"The Cask of Amontillado"

I finished those great last words, sighed, laid the book on my knees. Wind whirled a shroud of ash up the chimney. Scarlets and crimsons of the dying fire splashed its white column.

"*And now was acknowledged the presence of the Red Death,*" I murmured. "*He had come like a thief in the night. And one by one dropped the revellers in the blood-bedewed halls of their revel, and died each in the despairing posture of his fall. And the life of the ebony clock went out with that of the last of the gay. And the flames of the tripods expired. And Darkness and Decay and the Red Death held illimitable dominion over all.*"

"What'd you say? … I asked you a question…. It's that book, isn't it? You'll talk to that book, but will you bother to answer when I ask a polite question? Oh, no, I'm not important enough to deserve a reply."

The ghost in the chimney collapsed and fluttered down white over the red embers. Flakes dusted my bare feet. It was just ash, not a shroud-wrapped corpse dabbled with blood.

"I might as well talk to myself for all the notice you take. Why a civil question doesn't deserve a civil reply, I'll never understand. Night after night you sit reading

111

that book, not hearing a single word I say. It's not good enough."

"You sound more like my mother every day." I put the book on the mantelpiece, rolled up my swanny as a pillow, climbed into my sleeping bag, and blew out the candle.

"Why don't you read me one of them stories?" was the last complaint I heard from Harry Wakatipu, but I was already dreaming.

I dreamed of a walled abbey in the head of the Hopuruahine River. Of music falling from its towers across the miles of beech trees. Of a corpse that walked the bush in a white shroud dabbled with gore.

Halfway through the next morning, I climbed over the ridge behind the Orangitutaetutu, dropped into the Hopuruahine, crossed at the forks, worked into Dry Creek through the handy saddle, and sidled the Waioutukupuna faces down to the hut just after dark. I'd been cold and wet all day. There'd been a couple of deer in Dry Creek, that was all. The field officer would be on my hammer if I couldn't do better.

Water dripped and made a pool on the floor as I knelt. Lucky I'd hidden some kindling in my pack, or Harry Wakatipu would have burnt it. A brew would go down all right. My hands were so cold I couldn't pick out a single wax match. I spilled the lot on the hearth and fumbled one up. The red head crumbled with damp as I scratched it on the sandpaper along the side of the box. I fished up another, holding it between both hands, and struck it on the axe-head. The shavings caught, the kindling ignited. I split some light bits with my skinning knife, fed the growing flames, ran outside and dragged in rata logs.

I filled the billy from the spring and hung it in the torrent of flames. My wet swanny came off with a suck, and my socks. There was just time to throw in a handful of tealeaves, stand the billy on the hearth, shove the camp oven over the heat, and sit myself down before Harry Wakatipu got out of his sleeping bag and pinched my chair.

I kept the outside of my face straight, but grinned on the inside of my cheeks as he stood beside me and whined. "I've been waiting all day for someone to come home and get the fire going," he said. "I'm cold. I've not had a thing to eat."

I said nothing but took four deer kidneys from my pocket. Keeping my behind in my chair, I sliced the livers and hearts I'd carried home down the front of my bush singlet. I peeled and chopped a couple of onions, dropped the lot in the camp oven. It spat, hissed, and began turning them into hot, delicious tucker.

I poured a mug of tea, stirred in condensed milk with my skinning knife, and wiped it clean on my shorts before ramming it back in its sheath.

"What about me?"

"Me's been stinking on his bunk all day while real jokers have been out braving the elements. I've earned a brew." I took a long, noisy suck at my mug. "Is that good!" I muttered and sucked another mouthful through my whiskers: "Isssssssss!" My shorts were drying out already. My bush singlet would take longer, but it'd be okay before I went to bed. It was best to let woollen things dry on you, otherwise you got rheumatism, the field officer said.

"That chair will be sopping wet if you don't get up and change those wet things at once."

"Harry Wakatipu, not only do you sound like my mother; you're beginning to look like her." Still keeping in my chair I stirred the meat and onions around with my knife. In the heat my fingers tingled with pain. They were colder than I'd thought.

I set the lid off the camp oven upside-down on some embers, and flicked in a dab of butter. The baking powder was too far to reach without getting up from my chair, so I'd have to do without. I hooked a bag of flour out of the tucker cupboard, mixed a slurry of flour, milk powder, and water, and fried dollops on the red-hot lid. It only took them a few seconds to cook, and I crammed them down between gulps of hot tea. It's the quickest way to warm up, getting some buggers afloat inside you.

My fingers warm, I was ready to have a go at the camp oven. I topped up the tea billy and hung it back over the fire.

"Nobody ever thinks of old me. I could've drunk what was left in that billy."

"But you didn't, did you? So I've filled it up and hung it back over the fire, haven't I? In this life, Harry Wakatipu," I told the shivering pack-horse, "we don't lie around waiting for others to get the wood and water and light the fire and swing the billy. That's why you're standing there cold and sorry for yourself, and I'm sitting in my chair, full of hot tea and buggers afloat, and about to scoff a feed of liver, kidneys, hearts, and fried onions."

He stood shivering, miserable, waiting a chance to get his great rump down in my chair.

"Clear off, Hairy Legs. I don't want the pong of pack-horse in my tucker." He didn't move. I picked up a length of firewood. "Back off." He retreated to stand by the tucker cupboard. "Don't think you're going to fill up on condensed milk," I told him. "Rule Three says one tin per deer culler per day. Pack-horses don't get any."

I hooked a length of rata from the firewood box with my foot. It was a bit long but, if I stood to chop it through, that hairy brute would be into my chair, and I'd never get him out of it all night. Angled across the fireplace, the rata would burn okay.

I finished my second mug of tea, pulled the camp oven between my feet, and got stuck into the liver and kidneys, spearing them on a sharp stick. There was a fork on the table, but I didn't dare stand to reach it. We were out of spuds, and I'd have liked a bit of bread, but misery-guts had scoffed the whole of the loaf I'd baked last night. He loved camp oven bread dripping with condensed milk. His sleeping bag was always sticky with condensed milk. His hook-grass mattress was stuck together with it. No wonder the place ponged.

"That feels better!" I shoved the camp oven away and sprawled comfy in front of the fire. A couple of times up Dry Creek this afternoon I'd thought of throwing up a bivvy and sleeping out. I wondered what Harry Wakatipu would do. Just lie in his bunk, getting colder and colder, probably.

"Here." I kicked the camp oven towards him. "You can clean up what's left." For a few minutes there was the sordid din Harry Wakatipu kicks up when he's eating. "Knock it off," I told him. "It's bad for your heart, drinking all that fat. I've got to use that oven to cook my tucker in, and I don't want your dribble all over it."

He took the camp oven down from his mouth and sat on his ammunition case, back against the tucker cupboard. His next move would be to slip one hand inside and feel for a tin of condensed milk. I leaned and snibbed the padlock.

"Don't you trust me?"

"No!"

"It's not very pleasant knowing you're distrusted by your mate."

"You've lied and thieved since the day we came to the Hopuruahine. Why should I trust you?"

"Because we're mates."

"Mates look after each other. You can rely on your mate."

"You can rely on me!"

"The only thing I can rely on, Harry Wakatipu, is for you to pinch my chair, nick my bunk, and scoff my condensed milk."

Filled to the gizzard, I slept. When I woke, the rata log had burned through. Without leaving my chair, I kicked both ends on and looked around for my book. It was on the mantelpiece above the fireplace, but I couldn't reach it. Harry Wakatipu sat with the great swag of his puku between his knees, snoring and dribbling. He wasn't going to wake till the fire burned down and he got cold. Still, you never know with Harry Wakatipu. He's got the cheek of Ned Kelly when it comes to getting into my chair.

I scrutinised his face. Lack of exercise was making it flabby. There was a scar one side of his mouth where he'd cut it on a condensed milk tin. His mane was singed where he'd gone to sleep too close to the fire. The whiskers on his chin were shorter on one side where I cut them while he was asleep to see if it made him bump into things in the dark.

If I could just reach my book. *Tales of Mystery and Imagination* by Edgar Allan Poe. There wasn't a length of firewood long enough to knock it off the mantelpiece so I could fish it towards me and read another story. My rifle was too far away. And the axe was outside.

That had been a good feed. And the tea had been beaut. Matter of fact, I could do with another brew right now. I couldn't fill the billy, though, not without getting up, and that old misery was just waiting the chance to slip into my chair and go, "Hee haw! Hee haw!" Whenever I heard that hateful sound I knew I'd lost it.

I could pull the chair across towards the fire, close enough to reach my book, but Harry Wakatipu had his great feet stretched out, and he'd wake if I touched him. What was the name of the story I was going to read tonight? Last night's was "The Masque of the Red Death." Tonight's was going to be… What was it? I'd seen it when I finished the other last night. "The Cask of Amontillado." That was it.

Harry Wakatipu sagged against the tucker cupboard. He had a miserable sort of life, lying on his bunk all day, too lazy to cook himself a feed, waiting for me to come home and do it for him. Too tired to chop a bit of wood and keep the fire going. Too lazy to fetch a bucket of water and boil the billy. His own worst enemy. Nothing to look forward to but more years of lying in the dark inside the Hopuruahine hut, while other people got out and fought the elements like a man.

It was cold, getting going each morning. Once I'd been walking for a couple of hours my feet warmed up. If I walked with my rifle slung and my hands stuck down my crutch, they'd get warm, too. The only trouble was my crutch sometimes got cold instead. It's tough being a deer culler. But the world isn't meant to be easy, as I was always telling Harry Wakatipu. I'd told him again and again.

At least I'd got a couple of deer. I'd got out of the hut, got myself lost, and found my way home through the heavy cloud and dense bush. I was a tough-gutted deer culler. All I needed to finish off my day was to read "The Cask of Amontillado" and make a last brew of tea. I glanced sideways at Harry Wakatipu. Often I caught him looking at me from under his half-closed eyelids, but there was no movement this time. God, he was a noisy snorer.

Keeping my left hand on my chair, I reached out my right. I could almost touch the mantelpiece. Just a bit further and I could reach old Edgar Allan Poe. All I had to do was half stand, snatch the book, and drop back. I glanced at Harry Wakatipu, but he was out the monk. I stretched till my left hand lost touch with the chair, lifted my behind half an inch, silently, so it was no longer touching the seat. I straightened, snatched the book, and dropped back.

"Hee haw! Hee haw! Hee haw!"

I'd moved so fast, just the blink of an eye, but already he was sitting there. "Hee haw! Hee haw! Hee haw!" he went. "Hee haw! Hee haw!" It wouldn't have been so bad if he'd been silent.

"Get out of my chair at once!"

"I will not!"

"When I say get out, you get out!"

Harry Wakatipu hung on to the sides of the chair. He knew I'd never get him out of it. Well, horses are bigger, aren't they? And if I tipped him over, chair and all, he'd kick it to pieces. He'd done it before, and it took me ages to build a new one.

I said nothing. Dignifiedly, I took Edgar Allan Poe to my bunk. I took off my bush singlet, still a bit damp, and my shorts, and rolled them inside my swanny for a pillow that smelled of deer kidneys and livers. I got into my sleeping bag, lit the candle beside my bunk, and started to read "The Cask of Amontillado".

There was a clatter of feet and Harry Wakatipu was in his sleeping bag. "Read it aloud so I can hear?" He'd grizzle and keep me awake all night, if he didn't get his way.

"You've got the chair."

"I want a story."

"This isn't a very nice story. It'd scare you."

"I like scary stories!"

"You know they give you nightmares."

"They do not. Read it to me? Go on!"

There was nothing for it. Unless I blew out my candle and gave up reading for myself, he'd keep on all night. I opened the book at page 207 where "The Masque of

119

the Red Death" finished and read aloud the name of the next story: "The Cask of Amontillado."

"What's a cask?"

"Shut up and listen. It's a barrel."

"What's amontillado?"

"Do you want to hear this story or not?"

"Of course!"

"Then shut up and listen.

"*The thousand injuries of Fortunato I had borne as best I could,*" I read aloud, "*but when he ventured upon insult I vowed revenge.*"

"Ah!" Harry Wakatipu sighed.

When we got to the crypt with the human bones, Harry Wakatipu put his fingers in his ears and said, "I don't think I like this story."

"You insisted on hearing it. Now listen!" Harry Wakatipu began to snuffle. When I read the part where Montresor chained Fortunato against the wall, Harry Wakatipu's knees knocked together. I had to raise my voice.

"I don't like this story!"

I read on. When Montresor built the wall across the crypt, Harry Wakatipu sobbed, "I want to go to sleep."

"You promise you'll never pinch my chair again, and I'll stop reading aloud."

He was silent. I read a few more words aloud. "I agree! I agree!" Harry Wakatipu cried. "Just stop reading that terrible story."

I read silently to myself.

"What's happening?" asked Harry Wakatipu.

I went back and read from where I'd stopped.

"Stop! Stop! I don't want to hear any more! I promise I won't pinch your chair. I won't steal condensed milk. I won't answer back."

I read silently. It only took a few minutes.

"Is he letting Fortunato go?" asked Harry Wakatipu.

I read to myself.

"Tell me?" said Harry Wakatipu.

I read on silently.

"Read it aloud," said Harry Wakatipu, "or I take everything back. I'll pinch your chair and your bunk and your condensed milk. I won't light the fire or chop the wood or fetch the water. I'll– "

I finished reading the story aloud, and Harry Wakatipu shivered and cried. While I read the bit about the torch and the jingling of the bells, and putting the last brick in the wall, he tangied away like a waterfall. I finished the story and Harry Wakatipu sat up.

"Don't blow out the candle!"

"Act your age," I told him. "You're not a child."

"You blow out the candle, and I'll steal your condensed milk," he said. "I'll pinch your chair. I'll nick your bunk."

"What's new?" I blew out the candle, rolled over, and slept. Tomorrow, I'd take the boat and have a mooch around the lake. There were bound to be a few deer working out on the Marau clearings. It'd make a good change from the Hopuruahine and Harry Wakatipu. I'd take my book and read it without him bothering me.

"I hate you," said Harry Wakatipu. He was sitting up at the end of his bunk, scared I was going to build him in with a wall of bricks.

"I hate you, too," I said cheerfully. "Don't go to sleep, or somebody might creep in with bricks and mortar and start building you in."

"Ahhh!" he screamed. He'd sit there all night now, not able to get to sleep, listening for the sound of somebody laying bricks.

I chuckled and went to sleep. It served him right for pinching my chair. At least I think it served him right. What do you think? Of course it served him right. I'll bet you think so, too. Well it did, didn't it?

Chapter Seventeen
Shilly Shally and the Little Things

"*A gentleman* always stands when a lady comes into the room," my mother taught me. "Little things make all the difference," she said. My mother was a great one for saying, "A woman notices little things."

I was sitting in front of the fire in the Hopuruahine hut, one blazing hot summer's day, when there was a knock on the door. "Answer that," I told Harry Wakatipu.

"Answer it yourself."

"I order you to answer it."

Harry Wakatipu blew out his thick lips and sniggered. If I got up and answered the door he'd pinch my chair.

Knock, knock!

"I said, 'Answer that door.'"

"I said, 'You answer it yourself.'"

"You!"

"You!"

"You will so!"

"I will not!"

"Yes, you will."

"No, I won't."

"Yes, I will!" I said.

"Heh, heh, heh!" Harry Wakatipu sniggered. "You said,

'Yes, I will,' so you've got to open it. Heh, heh, heh!"

It's no good arguing with Harry Wakatipu. He knows our rule is that if I get up to open the door he's not allowed to pinch my chair. But he never plays fair. "What's the point having rules if you keep breaking them?" I ask him, but he just flaps his big lips and sniggers in that horrible way.

Knock, knock!

"Come in," I called, trying to sound pleasant.

"It won't open."

Harry Wakatipu waited for me to stand, every slack muscle in his flabby body ready.

"Pull the string," I called, "and raise the latch."

In came a woman dressed in the high boots and plumed hat of a government surveyor.

"Don't get up," she said as I rose to my feet, but I can't remain sitting when a woman enters the room. "They always say, 'Don't get up,'" said my mother, "but a gentleman always stands. Anyone who doesn't is beneath contempt."

Because I didn't want to be beneath the contempt of the visitor, I stood and took off my hat, something else my mother taught me.

"Heh! Heh! Heh!" I didn't need to look. Harry Wakatipu was already sitting in my chair. "Look after Number One!" he chortled, stretching his feet to the fire.

"It's hot in here," said the woman surveyor. "My name's Shilly Shally," she said. "I've been sent to survey the Vast Untrodden Ureweras. Who's that?"

"My pack-horse," I said, "Harry Wakatipu– " I was

about to say he was also the laziest, lying, bone-idle brute this side of the Northern Boundary. I was about to say he was beneath her contempt for not standing when she entered the hut. But Shilly Shally smiled, and my voice dried up.

Her lovely smile lit the darkest corner of the hut. Her eyes were blue as a kingfisher's wing in September, her hair yellow as kowhai around the Mokau flats in November, her lips scarlet as mistletoe on the beech trees around Lake Waikareiti in January. I tripped over the camp oven and knocked the tin basin off the table.

Her blue eyes opened wide. "I've heard so much about you!" She put out her hand. I raised mine, trembling, and Shilly Shally, still smiling her lovely smile, pushed past me and took Harry Wakatipu's hand. She didn't notice he hadn't stood and opened the door for her. She didn't notice he hadn't taken off his hat, my old hat he'd stolen from me. "I've always wanted to meet you, Mr Wakatipu!" I could hear her long eyelashes flapping up and down on her cheeks, and she was still hanging on to his hand.

"Beautiful Shilly Shally may be," I said under my breath, "but quite undiscriminating."

I boiled the billy, heated the stew, whipped up a batch of scones in the camp oven, and tried not to hear the disgusting palaver going on between Shilly Shally and Harry Wakatipu. When she knelt by my chair, held his front hoofs, and asked Harry Wakatipu if it was true he had chopped and sawn and split and slabbed and built the Hopuruahine hut all on his own, it was too much.

"Harry Wakatipu can pour a mug of tea for you," I

said. "Harry Wakatipu can tip out a plateful of stew for you. Harry Wakatipu can show you which bunk to use." Shilly Shally didn't hear a word I said. "You'll have to excuse me," I said in my most dignified voice, "but a man's got work to do."

I stuck a handful of bullets in my pocket and strode outside pulling on my swanny. It was a pity I'd forgotten my rifle. Blushing I strode back inside. The hut was nauseatingly hot. Shilly Shally's eyes – the colour of Radiant Blue ink – were turned upwards to Harry Wakatipu as he whinged about the hard time I gave him. I sucked in my stomach, stiffened my upper lip, and took my rifle. They didn't even notice me.

I rock-hopped up the Waioutukupuna bravely, sidled across the faces into Dry Creek manfully, and dropped into the right branch of the Hopuruahine courageously. Towards evening I swam down the river heroically. If Shilly Shally couldn't get the measure of that humbug, there was something wrong with her. "If a woman can't see through a scoundrel," my mother used to say about my father, "she needs her head read."

The hut was in darkness. Harry Wakatipu had burned all the firewood. I went out, chopped down a dead rata in the dark, felt for some dry tawa twigs, and got the fire going. Harry Wakatipu hadn't filled the water bucket so I took it outside to Hoho's spring. Harry Wakatipu had eaten all the bread, so I put on a loaf to bake in the camp oven. Harry Wakatipu had eaten all the stew, so I grilled some backsteaks on a forked stick.

Now there was a bit of light I could see Harry Wakatipu asleep on his own bunk for a change. Shilly

Shally lay on mine. She opened her dazzling blue eyes so they lit up the roof of the hut, revealing the thickets of cobwebs under the rafters. She saw me looking and said, "Mr Wakatipu told me you wouldn't mind if I used your bunk."

My mother taught me a gentleman always replies to a rhetorical question when it comes from a lady. I grunted politely.

Harry Wakatipu lay snoring on his back, all four feet in the air. "Try not to make too much noise," said Shilly Shally. "Poor Mr Wakatipu needs his sleep." She closed her eyes and plunged the hut into darkness.

Before first light next morning I had my gear packed, including the fresh loaf, and was off to shoot my way around the lake. By the time I got back, Shilly Shally should have learned her lesson. Perhaps she would wake up to Harry Wakatipu when she found he couldn't bake a loaf of bread, nor light a fire. When she found he couldn't put a stew together nor split a bit of firewood, she'd wish she'd been a bit more discriminating.

Several months later I got back. Harry Wakatipu sprang out the door as I arrived and cantered down the flats, neighing. On the table lay a carbon copy of a report written by Shilly Shally to the Surveyor-General in Wellington. She complained about the deer culler at the Hopuruahine hut for being rude and unco-operative. "Because the deer culler was not there to carry my pack and cook my bread, I was unable to survey the Vast Untrodden Ureweras," she wrote.

The field officer arrived from Ruatahuna. He had a copy of the report, too. I thought he'd fine me a couple of hundred bullets, but he counted my deer tails and laughed. "I saw her with her compass," he said. "She looked through it this way, and she looked through it that way. She didn't know which was north and which was south."

I thought he was being unfair. My mother always brought me up never to criticise a lady. "How are women to win equality," she used to ask, "if men are forever making stupid comments about unimportant trivia?"

"She shilly shallied for a couple of days," said the field officer, "and took off back to Wellington. She didn't know whether she'd be coming back." He laughed with typical male insensitivity. "I don't think she knew whether she was coming or going!" Had my mother been there she'd have given the field officer a flea in his ear for being rude about a lady.

"She had eyes blue as a kingfisher's wing in September," I said.

"What's that?"

"Her hair was yellow as the kowhais at the Mokau in November."

"Knock it off!"

"Her lips were scarlet as the mistletoe up at Waikareiti in January."

"You'd better read Rule Three in the Daybook again," said the field officer. "The one that says, 'Deer cullers must be kept ignorant about girls.'"

"Shilly Shally wasn't a girl. She was a lady."

"Lady is a vulgar genteelism for woman," said the field officer. He prided himself on being precise in his language now he had Biff Piddington to teach him.

"My mother said she was sure all women like to be thought of as ladies."

"I'll bet," said the field officer. "Anyway, Shilly Shally won't be back in a hurry. She also wrote a report about Harry Wakatipu. He never stood for her when she entered the hut. He took the best bunk and the best chair. He insisted on having the first mug of tea out of the billy, the first slice off every loaf of bread she baked, and the first spoonful out of every tin of condensed milk she opened. Why are you looking like that?"

"Nothing."

"Remember," said the field officer, "Rule Three in the Daybook says you're only allowed two grins a season, and one of them's gone!"

He burnt my deer tails and rode off to Ruatahuna. Harry Wakatipu sneaked back into the hut. I told him there was a bad report that said he didn't have enough manners even to stand for a lady. A few days later I told him he'd probably be sent down the road at the end of the season because he didn't stand when Shilly Shally came into the hut. Every day for the next few months, I reminded him about standing when a lady came into the hut.

At last the penny dropped, and Harry Wakatipu started leaping to his feet whenever he thought he heard a footstep outside. While he was sun-bathing by the river, all one day, I took the roof off the hut, sawed a couple of feet off the walls, and put the roof back on. As I expected, he didn't notice a thing.

Next morning I knocked lightly on the door. "Anybody in there?" I cooed in a high attractive voice. There was a terrible thump inside.

Harry Wakatipu lay unconscious, a lump as big as your fist between his ears where he'd stood up and knocked himself silly on a rafter, thinking a lady was coming into the hut.

Harry Wakatipu refuses now to stand for anyone when they come into the Hopuruahine hut. He has no manners. After knocking my own head on the roof a couple of times, I built it up again to its original height. That was several years ago, but Harry Wakatipu still goes round the hut bent over. You'd think he'd learn. Maybe it's because he's got no sense of humour. Still, what can you expect of a pack-horse?

Shilly Shally never came back. That's why the Ureweras have never been surveyed, why there's no maps of them still today. That's why there's no roads, no bridges, no towns, and no airports. If my mother hadn't brought me up to be polite to ladies, if I'd sat in my chair and not stood up for Shilly Shally, the Vast Untrodden Ureweras would be trodden and built all over, as boring as the rest of New Zealand.

"Little things make all the difference," my mother used to say, and I agree.

Chapter Eighteen
Teaching Harry Wakatipu to Bake Bread

"Why won't you teach me to bake bread?"

Hands white and soft from the dough I glared at the lying pack-horse sprawled in my chair. The field officer says you mustn't get angry with the dough or it won't rise. I ripped it in half. I pummelled and twisted it, punched it flat, flopped it over, and knocked it flat again. I kneaded into the dough the anger I felt. Sweat rolled off my forehead, ran down my nose, and a big drop fell on the dough. I rubbed with the heels of both palms and worked it in.

Teach him how to bake bread! For twenty years the Roman-nosed skullduggerer had complained about my scone loaves, raisin loaves, hot-cross buns, date scones, buggers afloat, and pikelets cooked on the inside of the camp oven lid. He complained about my milk powder bread that tasted like madeira cake; he complained about my saltless damper; he complained when there wasn't any bread because he'd gobbled the last of it. He complained there was too much yeast in it; he complained there wasn't enough; he complained when I made yeast from a potato bug. But in all those years of complaining he'd never had a go at making bread himself.

I rolled the dough into a ball and poked it. It pushed back, just the right amount of puffy resistance that tells you it's ready for rising.

"My mummy always used to give me a bit of dough when she was baking bread," whined Harry Wakatipu.

"It's not good for you."

"That's what you always say."

"You wouldn't like it."

"Yes, I would."

"I've given you bits before, and you didn't like it. I'm not wasting good dough on a pack-horse."

Harry Wakatipu climbed on his bunk, turned his long face to the wall, and grizzled. "Ooooh, hoo! Ooooh hoo!"

I placed the dough in the warmed camp oven, put on the lid gently, and tiptoed away. By the time the dough rose and filled the camp oven, the matai would have burnt to big coals, just right for shovelling on the lid.

"Ooooh hoo! Ooooh hoo!" Harry Wakatipu stopped and listened in case I'd sneaked outside. You'd think he'd be embarrassed when he finds he's been grizzling to an empty hut, but Harry Wakatipu just tangies louder. I've even seen him come outside, look around, come over and stand beside me, and start grizzling there. "Ooooh hoo!" he goes. "Ooooh hoo!" If ever a sound gets on my nerves it's that one.

The tuis around the Hopuruahine sometimes get sick of copying the sound of my cross-cut and try to copy Harry Wakatipu grizzling, but they can't get that loopy "oooh" sound into their voices, thank goodness. The morepork who lives in the hollow rata sometimes gives a "Hoo-hoo" that sounds close to it, but he always goes back to his "More-pork! More-pork!"

I made a brew of tea and sat, sweat running down my face. Harry Wakatipu notched his grizzling higher.

"Knock it off, will you?"

"Ooooh hoo! Ooooh hoo!"

I took my mug outside and sat on the wood heap. The Waiotukupuna was dirty from the big slip. The Hopuruahine looked bright blue beside it. A long-tailed cuckoo gave its mad squawk. Cicadas shrilled in the kanukas by the pool below the hut. Later I'd tie one of those woolly flies with a hair out of Harry Wakatipu's tail and a wisp out of my swanny. I'd make it look like a cicada and try to fool the old brownie who'd been making an idiot of me every season for the past twenty years.

"Ooooh hoo! Ooooh hoo!" Harry Wakatipu had sneaked behind me. "Ooooh hoo! Ooooh hoo!"

"You should be ashamed of yourself, carrying on like a two-year old. Why should I teach you to make bread? For over twenty years I've been asking you to do it, but it didn't suit you, not Harry Wakatipu!"

Suddenly I realised why he'd followed me. I ran inside and lifted the lid. Somebody had kicked the side of the camp oven, and the dough had gone flat.

Harry Wakatipu stuck his long head inside the door. When I looked up he hid his grin and started "Ooooh hoo-ing" again.

"Of all the low-down tricks…" I tipped the flattened dough back into the tin basin, and kneaded it again. Fortunately there was still life in the yeast. In a few minutes I had it as good as ever, back in the camp oven, rising again.

"You left the camp oven in the middle of the floor. It wasn't my fault I tripped over it."

"You did it on purpose. If Biff Piddington was here, he'd show you!" I stuttered with rage and stepped outside. Bread doesn't rise when you're in a bad mood. Dough likes thundery weather, but not thundery tempers, the field officer always says.

I split some matai to make more coals. And Harry Wakatipu picked it up. He actually picked up some firewood and carried it inside! In twenty years I'd never seen him lower himself to carry a single bit of firewood. Now he hopped in the door with an armload.

"Oh, sorry!" There was a clang from the camp oven. He'd dropped a lump of matai on the lid. I didn't need to take it off to know the bread was finished; the yeast wasn't that good.

"You've pakarued it this time." I took the dough to the pool below the hut, where the big brownie lay on the surface and swallowed bits as I threw them, opening his great gob till I could see halfway down his throat. "I hope it gives you indigestion," I told him.

There was no way I could bake bread. Even if I locked Harry Wakatipu outside he'd crawl underneath and kick the floor to stop it rising. He once let off a stick of gelignite behind the hut and flattened the bread I was baking. He reckoned he was making a new rubbish hole. Another time he stuck a handful of blasting powder in the fireplace. I was beaten, and he knew it.

"I give in, Harry Wakatipu. I'll teach you to bake bread."

"I knew you'd see things my way!"

134

"Tell me, after all these years, why do you want to learn to make bread? What made you change your mind?"

"It was the sweat running down your nose, and dripping into the dough. And you kneaded it into the bread I was going to have to eat."

"Come off it, Harry Wakatipu! Everyone sweats as they knead dough."

"I'd rather eat my own sweat than somebody else's, thank you very much."

"Oh, lahdy dah!"

"There's no need to go that way."

"You've got the cheek of Ned Kelly, you have, Harry Wakatipu.

"Build up the fire so you'll have some coals," I said. "Warm the basin, and chuck in about three or four double handfuls of flour."

He warmed the tin basin, put in the flour and a bit of salt, and left it in front of the fire.

"Put three lidfuls of yeast in about half a small billy of warm water with a tablespoon of sugar."

"I'll use condensed milk," said Harry Wakatipu, "instead of the sugar."

I should have thought of it before. Honey, sugar, jam, beer, konini berries, Harry Wakatipu had seen me use them all. Anything sweet would get the yeast working. The cunning old skinflint, he'd thought he'd open a new tin of cond, stir a couple of spoonfuls in with the yeast, and scoff the rest. Well, I was one jump ahead of him. I grinned to myself.

"You're not getting into the condensed milk again.

Now, put the billy near the fire. Not too close or you'll kill the yeast. Give it about ten minutes to work, and start mixing it into your flour. You've seen me do the rest often enough. Knead the yeast into the dough, set it to rise in the camp oven, and hang it over the fire.

"Shove your hoof under the camp oven and count to ten, that's how hot it should be. Shovel a good heap of coals on the lid. And give it about an hour."

I'd fobbed him off with a pretty hairy sort of recipe. It would do for a pack-horse who was only good for dog-tucker, anyway. I wasn't giving him my great-grandfather's secret recipe for bread. It called for half-a-dozen tins of condensed milk, and that would have been right up Harry Wakatipu's alley.

In any case I knew he'd lose interest and give it away. He never sticks at anything long enough to make a go of it. Specially now he wasn't going to get a tin of cond. I'd take it over, finish kneading it properly, and put it on to bake. It's not in Harry Wakatipu's nature to see anything through. Who ever heard of a pack-horse baking bread?

Chapter Nineteen
My Side of the Hut

I **came home** from a fly-camping trip through the Ruakituri where the trees grew so close together it was dark at midday. Back at the Hopuruahine I kept my eyes half-closed for a couple of weeks before they got used to the dazzle.

Once there was Biff Piddington, then there was Wiki, and then there was Hoho. Now there was just me and Harry Wakatipu at the Hopuruahine. All the months I'd been away he hadn't bothered to light the fire once. He lived on condensed milk and cold baked beans. No wonder he stunk. Even with the fire going, it'd take a couple of weeks to air the hut and get rid of his pong.

One thing, though, my tail-line was full. The field officer never admits I've been working well. He just gives a little nod as he counts and destroys the deer tails, and I know I'm doing all right. You have to be very quick to see his nod. He tries to give it with his back to you or when you're looking away. Sometimes several years go by without my knowing whether I'm doing all right or not.

I once came across an old deer culler dying alone in the bush up the head of the Hopuruahine. He said his field officer used to say, "Near enough," or, "She'll be right," when he shot a big tally. Things must have been easier then.

I made the old chap a billy of tea. "Remember Rule Three in the Daybook, 'A deer culler must never get up himself,'" he said. I left a tin of condensed milk open beside him and kept going. Rule Three also says, "A real joker doesn't waste sympathy on a hopeless case."

Now, although I was quite pleased with my tail-line, I remembered the old chap's advice and didn't get up myself. Still, it would have been nice to have someone say I was doing all right. I could have done with a bit of company.

You wouldn't call Harry Wakatipu company. I thought back to the time years ago when I built the Hopuruahine hut, and Harry Wakatipu started taking over. He pinched my chair in front of the fire. He nicked my bunk. He stole my condensed milk. He wanted everything.

I decided enough was enough this time when I got back from the Ruakituri. "You're not just a liar and a thief," I told Harry Wakatipu. "Your trouble is you're always getting up yourself."

"Look after Number One I always say," said Harry Wakatipu. He gave his irritating snigger, "Heh, heh, heh." If I've asked him once I've asked him a thousand times not to snigger, but nothing I say makes any difference. I should never have let him see how much it annoys me.

It's different when it comes to his own gear. Like the time his mother sent him a birthday cake. Next morning there were crumbs all over his saddle blanket. I accused him of scoffing it on his own, and he said I'd just imagined a birthday cake. He swore his mother always forgot his birthday. He grinned and gave that irritating snigger, "Heh, heh, heh!", and I saw the pink icing stuck between his teeth, and the hundreds and thousands his mother had used to write, "Happy Birthday Harry Wakatipu" on his cake.

I'm not allowed to touch his smelly old saddle blanket, yet he's always trying to sneak off with my swanny. If I forget for a moment and sit on his bunk, he rushes over, sits beside me, and shoves along till I move. Yet just about every night he climbs on to my bunk and pretends he's asleep when I tell him to clear off.

This time when I got back from the Ruakituri I found he'd been wearing my new bush singlet, my best swanny, and my spare boots. He'd been smoking my pipe, and drinking condensed milk out of my mug. I didn't see why I should put up with it any longer.

I took a lump of charcoal from the fire and drew a line across the floor. "That's your side of the hut, Harry Wakatipu. And this is mine. From now on you keep to your side, and I'll keep to mine."

Harry Wakatipu climbed on to his bunk and sulked. He's always doing that. He sticks out his bottom lip, turns to the wall, and grizzles. At least while he's sulking he's not pinching my condensed milk.

I baked a loaf of bread, cooked a stew, and swung the billy. I sat in my chair on my side of the fireplace, heaped my plate with my stew, filled my mug with my tea, and cut myself a slice of my bread. Harry Wakatipu's long head looked around the corner of his bunk when he smelled my condensed milk.

He snatched up the charcoal and brayed, "Let's divide everything equally!" He tried to draw a black line of charcoal down the side of the black billy. He drew a

139

line across the bread. He drew a line across the lid of the camp oven. "And the table," he gibbered. "And the door. And the window. And the tucker cupboard."

"Lay off," I said. "That's my tucker cupboard. Horses eat mahoe."

"You said everything was to be divided in two." He drew lines down the handles of the axe and the broom. He drew a line down the back of my chair. "Everything!"

"That's my chair."

"You said everything!" He drew a line down the middle of my bunk. He drew lines down the middle of my swanny, my bush singlet, my socks, my boots. Everything in the hut, Harry Wakatipu divided in two.

I should have known you can't talk sense to a pack-horse. Now, when I try to sit on my chair, Harry Wakatipu gallops across and sits on his side of it. When I put on my swanny, Harry Wakatipu tries to push into his side. When I pour a mug of tea he reckons I'm tipping it out of his side of the billy. He watches to see I don't cut a slice of bread off his side. When I go to the dunny, he pushes inside and watches to see I don't use his side of the seat. I hate anyone watching, so now I always go when I'm up in the bush. That's not much fun because it rains all the time at the Hopuruahine.

As I said to Harry Wakatipu, it's silly, taking things too literally. He sniggered, "Heh, heh, heh!" and flapped his lips. "You were the one who divided the hut in two."

I don't know why I bother. It's a waste of time trying to make Harry Wakatipu understand anything. This morning I forgot and used his side of the door, and he was on his feet at once, shouting and pointing. Then he had to use my side of the door to make up. It might be easier to build another hut at the Hopuruahine and let Harry Wakatipu have the old one. He can pong all he likes and let it get dirty and untidy. The only trouble is I might come home from a fly-camp somewhere up the back of beyond and find he's moved in and claimed half of mine.

There's times I wish I'd never seen the half-witted brute. The trouble is he's got no sense of humour. He can never see anyone else's point of view. I wonder if that's what Rule Three means about a deer culler never getting up himself?

Chapter Twenty
Christmas at the Hopuruahine

"*Are we having* a Christmas tree this year?"

I stared at Harry Wakatipu.

"I said are we having a Christmas tree this year?"

"I heard the first time. What do you mean are we having a Christmas tree?"

"I want a Christmas tree, you know with bits of cottonwool, and a star on top, and a stocking hanging by the fireplace for Santa Claus to climb down the chimney and fill with presents. I want carols and everyone being nice to me for Christmas. I've never had a Christmas. Ooooh hoo!" He tangied away.

If there's one thing I can't stand, it's Harry Wakatipu grizzling. Besides I felt a bit guilty. I'd tried to keep Christmas a secret from him, just as my mother kept it a secret from me until I heard the other kids at school talking about it. I said nothing to him but threw some gear into my pack, grabbed some ammo, and took off up the Waiotukupuna.

"He knows perfectly well that real jokers don't believe in Father Christmas," I grumbled aloud as I climbed the Big Slip. I'd drop over the back of the ridge, and spend a few weeks mooching through the creek-riddled

Mokau watershed. That should take my mind off Christmas. By the time I got back to the Hopuruahine, Harry Wakatipu would have forgotten it, too.

Rule Three in the Daybook says the field officer must tell his deer cullers Father Christmas isn't true, that any deer culler caught whistling carols will get the sack, and anyone who hangs up a stocking will get sent down the road. "A real joker," Rule Three says, "won't even know it's Christmas. He'll be out in the bush, fly-camping."

I camped that night under a rotten log in a wet creekhead. At least I didn't have to go far for water. "Christmas?" I said aloud. "What's Christmas?"

At Ruatahuna, the other side of the Huiarau Range, the field officer was allowed to have a Christmas. As I tried to light a fire with wet crown-fern I thought of my friends Wiki, Biff Piddington, and Hoho McKenzie. On Christmas Eve they'd light candles and walk singing carols down the track from the base-camp, through the horse paddock, to Russ and Pat Tulloch's place. They'd go singing to Iti's, and Mak's, and down to Pakitu's. Then, candles burnt out, they'd trot home, hang up their stockings, and go to bed wondering what Santa Claus was going to bring them.

They'd wake early on Christmas morning and feel in the dark for their stockings. They'd make a row playing with their presents and wake the field officer. He'd grumble but get up and light the fire and boil the plum duff. They'd have thick yellow custard and find threepences and half-crowns in the Christmas pudding. Biff Piddington would make Christmas crackers out of covers off the *Auckland Weekly News*, and they'd go bang

143

with the grains of blasting powder he put inside. Wiki whose father was German would sing "Heilige Nacht" in her high, true voice. Hoho would tell her famous story about kindly old Uncle Scrooge and his mean nephew, Bob. Everyone would cry when she told the sad bit about Tiny Tim winning the Art Union and refusing to share it with the rest of his family.

For several weeks I tramped through the bush, trying not to think about Christmas and my friends at the base-camp. The trouble was the field officer always told me about Christmas each year after it was over.

"I don't like to think of you on your own out in the wet bush on Christmas Day. I'm too soft-hearted for my own good," he always said.

"Thank you for telling me," I always said back to him.

He smiled modestly. "I'll feel better about it next Christmas Day," he said. "At least I'll know you're thinking about us having a good time while you're out there wet-through, lost, and lonely in the never-ending unmapped bush of the Vast Untrodden Ureweras."

"You are too kind," I used to say to him. It pays to keep on good terms with your field officer.

But I was telling you about that fly-camping trip. There were hardly any deer. It's lifeless beech country, the Mokau, with only the occasional pied tit and grey robin hopping along the ground. Branches interlocked, kept out the light, and dripped. I hadn't seen the sky since leaving the top of the Big Slip. My swanny was growing moss, and the back of my neck was sprouting toadstools when, one wet day, I climbed out of the muddle of dirty gullies and log-jammed creek-heads and dropped

144

over the watershed into the top of the Waioutukupuna. I dived into the gorge and swam downstream for several weeks, camping the night on sandbanks and swimming on. One morning I heard a roar and grabbed hold of a rock just in time to stop myself going over the Waiotukupuna waterfall.

If I jumped down the waterfall I could reach the Hopuruahine that night. If I took the careful way and climbed down it would take a couple more days. The trouble is the waterfall bulges out at the top, so you can't see the pool at the bottom, but it's quite safe really. It's deep. The only trouble is it's a bit narrow, and the boulders along both sides are white with the bones of deer cullers who were in too much of a hurry to get to the hut. They jumped off without making sure where they were going to land.

If you jump with your pack on, its weight turns you upside-down so you fall headfirst, and you're in trouble. I strapped my rifle to my pack, threw it out over the edge. I stood in the creek so my boots filled up, tied tight the lace at the neck of my swanny, took a bit of a run, and sailed out over the lip of the waterfall.

The water in my boots made me fall feet first. Between them I could see my pack, a tiny dot like this • drifting down below me. It had about another half hour before it landed. I grabbed the tail of my swanny and held it open so it filled with air and lowered me like a parachute. (Not many people know that's why swannies have long tails.) I saw the white fleck as my pack and rifle splashed into the pool. I'd take a couple more hours to get there. You can do it faster. Once, I forgot to do up

145

the lace on my swanny, the air rushed out of the neck, and I came down in under an hour. My feet hit the water so hard I had to wear boots two sizes larger after that. What you learn to do is to lift the tail of your swanny and let out a bit of air so you slip sideways. That way you can save a bit of time and choose where you're going to land.

I circled and looked at the blue ducks who live half-way down. A couple of younkers got scared and fell out of the nest, but they swam back up the face of the water-fall, whistling their name, "Whio! Whio!" and running their tongues over their jagged teeth to make that ratchety noise.

An hour or so later I sideslipped into the pool beside my pack and tramped on. Near the mouth of the Waiotukupuna I tipped the water out of my rifle barrel and shot a decent-sized trout, big enough to feed my-self and Harry Wakatipu. Slung over my shoulder, its head touched the ground in front, and its tail dragged on the ground behind. Lucky it was close to the hut because it was fairly heavy.

Harry Wakatipu was sitting on the chopping block trying to get a branch of tea-tree to stand up in a con-densed milk tin. He'd polished some other tins, chopped them into bits, and hung them glittering on the tea-tree. One tin he'd chopped into the shape of a star and tied it on top.

"What do you think you're doing?"

"It's me Christmas tree," he said. "Tonight's Christ-mas Eve." I felt a sudden tenderness for the brute. He's only a pack-horse after all, so how could he know real

146

jokers don't believe in Father Christmas?

"All right," I barked gruffly so he wouldn't think I was giving in. "Just this once I'll boil you a tin of condensed milk for Christmas, the way you like it, but don't think this is going to become a habit."

I stood on his back and lowered the trout down the chimney to smoke, and put a tin of cond in a billy of water and began boiling it. Harry Wakatipu loves cond at the best of times, but he goes mad when it's boiled for several hours and whacked into lollies he can suck. He's what Biff Piddington calls "oral-fixated", Harry Wakatipu.

Anyway we were sitting in front of the fire, and Harry Wakatipu was dribbling and poking at the billy with a stick. "Leave it alone, will you?" I told him. "It's not going to boil any faster because you keep looking at it." And I stopped and listened. You hear all sorts of noises at the Hopuruahine because of the high walls around it, the steep faces off the ridges. Some of those gullies have trapped noises that go back a couple of hundred years. Stand and whisper by the big rock across the river, and anyone inside the hut will turn white with what they hear. I've often done that to Harry Wakatipu, just to stir him up when he's feeling a bit down.

Anyway we were sitting there, and I heard something like water pouring over a high waterfall, a trickle of liquid silver that fell and fell and then sort of turned and climbed up again, if a trickle of silver-sounding water can climb uphill. Suddenly I realised what a fountain must sound like in the middle of the desert. It reminded me of something I once heard before I ran away from

147

home to escape my mother. I thought I could smell that sharp scent you get off pine trees, especially when there's snow around. I coughed because there was something tickling in my throat and, do you know, that old fool of a Harry Wakatipu was blubbing? Can you believe it? Sitting blubbing in front of the fire in the Hopuruahine hut!

It's as well he's just a pack-horse and not a deer culler. Rule Three in the Daybook says, "Any deer culler caught crying will be sacked. His rifle barrel will be bent. The blade on his skinning knife will be snapped. And he will be dogged out of the Vast Untrodden Ureweras for the rest of his natural life."

"Pull yourself together, Harry Wakatipu!" I told him sternly. I stirred up the fire, not too much because of our trout up the chimney. I sat back in my chair and heard the high, pure sound again. It started the whole valley ringing like crystal until something rang inside me and I felt as if I would snap in half. "There's something funny going on," I said gruffly. I got up and wandered over to the door to give Harry Wakatipu a chance to pull himself together. Nothing embarrasses me more than a man who can't control his emotions. I looked up the valley.

In the gloom below the Cascades, where the track zigzags down a thousand feet to the Hopuruahine hut, a line of lights came bobbing. Wiki, and Biff Piddington, and Hoho McKenzie riding a string of pack-horses. Holding candles above their heads. Singing "Silent Night". Wiki's high true soprano clear above the others, only she was singing in German because her father was a Hun. Her voice laced the cold night air. Like falling water.

The pack-horses were loaded with chaff sacks full of Christmas presents. One carried a freshly-cut pine tree. The field officer rode at the back, dressed as Father Christmas. I knew it was him because he was wearing the spurs he'd perked off me. "Real jokers don't wear spurs," he'd said as he confiscated them.

"You've got your wish," I told Harry Wakatipu, "though I don't know what you've done to deserve it." We were all together again for Christmas, one big happy family. Even the field officer. There'd be presents. We'd cook a plum duff. Biff would make us some Christmas crackers with the gelignite I kept under my bunk. Hoho would tell us the story of her uncle and his nephew and Tiny Tim's Art Union ticket. We'd all eat so much we'd fall asleep after Christmas dinner.

"Don't go expecting this to happen every year," I told Harry Wakatipu, but he didn't hear a word I said. He was too busy gawping at Father Christmas, listening to him going, "Ho! Ho! Merry Christmas, Harry Wakatipu!", and sniffing at the chaff sacks for condensed milk.

"Merry Christmas!" I called and ran to hold the head of Wiki's horse. "Merry Christmas, Wiki, and Biff Piddington, and Hoho! Merry Christmas, Santa Claus!" I turned. "Come on!" I hissed. "Help them off their horses and wish them Merry Christmas!" But do you know that great booby was standing there bawling his eyes out and making them worse by rubbing them with his front feet? He's not got a single manly bone in his body, Harry Wakatipu. He lets down the side every time.

I'd like to finish the story here. Leave it with us all sitting in front of the fire in the Hopuruahine hut on

149

Christmas Eve. Wiki's singing her song. The field officer's remembering to say, "Ho! Ho!" every now and again. Biff Piddington's enormous head is nodding in time to the music. Hoho's about to tell us her story. I'd like to finish here. I don't really want to tell you the rest of it.

I don't want to tell you how the field officer got up in the dark, dressed as Father Christmas, and was filling Harry Wakatipu's enormous stocking with tins of condensed milk, and Harry Wakatipu thought it was a thief and bit his behind so hard the field officer leapt and got stuck up the chimney beside the smoked trout. By the time I got him down, his whiskers were burnt off and he was pretty well smoked himself. He was all set to start straight back to Ruatahuna, but I swung the billy, made a brew of tea, and quietened him. Then he wanted to arrest me for shooting trout.

I don't want to tell you how Harry Wakatipu set fire to the Christmas tree when he climbed up it to steal everyone else's Christmas presents. I don't want to tell you how he fell in the Christmas pudding when I offered him a stir, and he tried to eat the whole thing himself and pinched all the threepences and half-crowns out of it. We had to pick his hairs out of our slices before we could eat it.

I don't want to tell you how Harry Wakatipu pulled all the Christmas crackers by himself, tore up the paper hats, and got drunk. If it'd been me I'd have got the bullet. It's a sacking offence, having booze on a deer block. It's not fair, the way the field officer lets Harry Wakatipu get away with things.

I don't want to tell you how Harry Wakatipu made

himself sick with all the condensed milk he drank and wet his sleeping bag because he was too scared to go outside before he went to bed.

I don't want to tell you any of those things. I think it's better if I keep them quiet because most of all Christmas is a time for forgiving and forgetting. It says so in the Daybook.

On the morning of Boxing Day, Harry Wakatipu woke from his snoring as the others were about to ride back to Ruatahuna. He galloped out of the hut and yelled at the field officer, "Are we having another Christmas next year?"

"Over my dead body!" said the field officer. He sat in the saddle sideways, his behind still sore. His hair and eyelashes were singed down one side where he'd been jammed up the chimney with the smoked trout. Biff Piddington said something to him.

"Well," said the field officer, "maybe Wiki, and Biff Piddington, and Hoho might come back for Christmas next year, but you needn't go expecting to see Father Christmas again, not after what you did to him Christmas Eve."

They rode up the track. I waved. They disappeared into the clouds. Silence fell on the Hopuruahine. The hut seemed very small amongst the thousands and thousands of miles of trees that blanket the hills and ridges and ranges of the Vast Untrodden Ureweras.

"I'm going fly-camping," I said distantly, but Harry Wakatipu didn't hear me. He was playing with a Meccano set Father Christmas had brought him. He'd already counted his tins of condensed milk and hidden them from me. "Look after Number One!" Harry Wakatipu always says.

I tied the rope around the neck of my pack, stuck some ammo in the back pocket, poked the tongue through an eyelet and down through the buckle. As I dropped the pack outside the door, Harry Wakatipu said, "When's the next Christmas?"

I got my rifle from behind the door.

"I said, 'When's the next Christmas?'"

I took out the empty magazine.

"Are we having another Christmas next year?" asked Harry Wakatipu.

I filled the magazine and thought of the hours I'd spent arranging Christmas, the time I'd spent cooking and working my fingers to the bone just so that old brute would have a happy time, and I wondered if it's worth it. If he thinks I'm working like that just so he can get drunk and bite Father Christmas and burn down the Christmas tree, well he's got another think coming.

"Certainly not!" I swung up my pack.

"Ooooh hoo!" he started grizzling.

I smacked the magazine into my rifle and strode off into the bush. "We'll see," I muttered, not loud enough for Harry Wakatipu to hear.